BEFORE You

the SEX ON THE BEACH series

the SEX ON THE BEACH series

Jenna Bennett

This is a work of fiction. Names, characters, places and incidents either are the product of the author's imagination or are used fictitiously, and any resemblance to actual persons, living or dead, business establishments, events or locales is entirely coincidental.

Photograph: Sergey P.
Cover Design: Sarah Hansen, OkayCreations.com
Interior Design: E.M. Tippetts Book Design

ISBN: 978-0-9899434-6-8

Magpie Ink

Dear Reader,

Prepare yourself for Sex on the Beach, a trilogy featuring BETWEEN US (Jen McLaughlin), BEYOND ME (Jennifer Probst), and BEFORE YOU (Jenna Bennett). Three separate novellas. Three different authors. One literary world. Read them all, or just read one. It's up to you! No matter which route you choose, these standalone novellas are sure to satisfy your need for sizzling romance and an emotion packed story.

Happy Reading!
Jen, Jenna, and Jennifer

Praise for BEFORE YOU:

"The story felt fun, as Cassie enjoys the sunshine, and things develop and start to sizzle when she meets Ty. It kept me on the edge of my seat...and I was curling my toes at the romance." *–Bella, from A Prairie Girl Reads*

"A thrilling mystery mixed with romance and some much needed humour and wittiness, BEFORE YOU is an enjoyable and gripping story." *–Stella, Ex Libris*

Praise for BEYOND ME:

"I loved this book, I very much enjoyed getting to know James and Quinn, and I wanted to step into their world of sun and water and love. This book made spring break even more fun, even with the intense feelings, I want to head to Florida now! I give this book 5 huge sunny and sandy stars!" *–Sizzling Book Blog*

"Jennifer Probst does it again in BEYOND ME with another amazing hit. From the first chapter I was captivated immediately and couldn't put it down. The chemistry between James and Quinn had my heart racing, soaring, and dropping on more than one occasion. I found myself lost in their story, not wanting it to end." *–NYT & USA Today Bestselling Author Kelly Elliott*

Praise for BETWEEN US:

"The sweet good-girl looking to be a bit naughty and the sexy bad-boy looking to be thought of as good…Jen gives us another winning story with BETWEEN US. Drool worthy and devourable with plenty of emotion, I adored this book from start to finish! A must read!" *–Jillian, from Read, Love, Blog*

"Anything that Jen McLaughlin writes is gold, in my book. BETWEEN US is no different. Set in the sweltering heat of Key West, it has all the passion, friendship and drama that made it impossible to put down. Go read this book. You won't be disappointed!" *–Casey, Literary Escapism*

It's all fun and games

I had a simple plan for spring break.

Sun, sand, and a hot guy. Sex on the beach with no strings attached.

A chance to get rid of this pesky virginity once and for all.

And when I met Tyler McKenna, I thought I had it made.

Until someone gets hurt

But then girls started turning up at Key West landmarks. Girls who looked like me, but with one crucial difference: They'd all been drugged and relieved of their virginity.

The virginity I still have. The virginity Ty refuses to take.

And now I've begun to wonder whether there isn't more to him than meets the eye.

Suddenly, sex on the beach doesn't sound so good anymore...

For Jen and Jennifer, or Jennifer and Jen.
It's been great working with you.
Here's to much success, and the chance to do it again!

CHAPTER *One*

This was the life. Sun, sand, and hot guys, plus an unlimited supply of alcohol, thanks to Mackenzie Forbes, who was bound and determined that her friends have a good time.

Spring break in Key West. What could be better?

I put my half-empty glass on the bar and turned to survey the room.

It was only Sunday night. We'd been here just over twenty-four hours, and Mackenzie had already homed in on the guy she'd decided to spend the week with. He was local, not one of the college guys down for spring break. Older than us by a few years, and dressed in ripped jeans with tattoos visible under his shirt. All the things America's Sweetheart should stay far away from, but didn't.

Looking at Mackenzie, I was very glad I was just plain Cassie Wilder from Nowheresville, Ohio. Fame and fortune sound great on paper, but try losing your virginity with the paparazzi breathing down your neck. Try falling in love and having your relationship splattered all over the tabloids.

Try breaking up and having everyone in America weighing in on whether he cheated or you did, and how you're coping with being dumped again.

No thanks. If Mackenzie had found a guy who wasn't gonna sell her out to the press, more power to her.

Quinn had already left, with some Ivy League dude hot on her trail.

He'd been staring at her for an hour, from the table where he'd been sitting with his friends, and when she got up to go, he took off after her. Neither of them had come back, so either he'd talked her into going somewhere with him, or she'd made it back to the hotel in one piece and was up in her room spending quality time with her television boyfriend. With Quinn, it could be either.

That left me here by myself.

Luckily, there were still plenty of guys to choose from, and plenty of time left. Key West was stuffed to the gills this week, and I had five and a half days of vacation to go.

This was it. I was going to find a guy and join Quinn among the ranks of the devirginized.

The Ivy Leaguers didn't appeal, though. Nor did the guys with tattoos. And I'm not that big on jocks. It didn't leave a whole lot of options.

I turned back to my glass. But before I could reach for it, someone whisked it away. "How about I get you a fresh drink?"

It went into the hand of the bartender, who carried it away.

The guy who had spoken had green eyes and hair that straddled the line between dark blond and light brown. The streaks through the front could have been sun, or just expensive highlights. He was wearing jeans—good quality but not designer, faded but not ripped—and a navy blue T-shirt, one that said *FBI* in big white letters across the chest. I had to lean closer to see that below, in much smaller letters, it said *Female Body Inspector.*

"Nice shirt," I said.

He glanced down and up again. "Thanks. I'm Ty."

Good name. Cute guy. Sense of humor. Check, check, and check.

I smiled. "Cassandra Wilder. Wanna inspect my body?"

He grinned. "Maybe later. Where d'you blow in from, Cassie?"

"Chicago," I said. "University of. You?"

"Washington."

"State?"

He shook his head. "D.C. But I'm from Florida originally."

"Key West?"

"Jacksonville. North Atlantic coast."

"I'm from Ohio," I said. "Small town in the middle of nowhere. Lots of cornfields and cows. Chicago's a lot more exciting."

"Sounds like." He folded his arms on the bar. Nice arms. Nice smile. Good teeth and a dimple. "So how long have you been in Key West?"

I told him we'd flown down the day before and arrived in the afternoon. "We've been here about," I checked my watch, "thirty-two hours."

"You come down with friends?"

I nodded. "There are three of us. Mackenzie is over there in the corner. Quinn already left."

His brows lowered at that. "Alone?"

"She had some guy following her. Part of that group over there." I pointed to where some of Ivy League Dude's friends—just as Ivy League, Abercrombie and Fitch all the way—were still hanging out, knocking back shots of tequila like there was no tomorrow.

Ty watched for a second and then turned back to me. "How long ago did they leave?"

"I don't know. Twenty minutes? Why?"

He shrugged. "No reason. There's a lot of people in town this week. Safer not to go off alone."

"She wasn't alone. Ivy League Dude followed her."

He tilted his head, and a hank of blond hair fell across his forehead. "But she doesn't know Ivy League Dude, does she?"

"Same way I don't know you," I said.

Dammit, was he just talking to me as an excuse to find out about Quinn? I mean, I know she's pretty and all, but I'm not that bad. Am I?

He grinned. "Wanna see my driver's license?"

"I'll show you mine if you'll show me yours."

"Deal." He fished in his back pocket and pulled out a wallet. I dipped my fingers into my mini-purse and pulled out all the glossy cards, sorting them on the counter.

"Room key, credit card, license." I pushed the license toward him.

He picked it up. "Nice picture."

Not so much. Official photographs are rarely that good. And I'd had a zit on my chin that day. Although the picture was so small it didn't matter too much, I supposed.

I looked at his. Tyler Jackson McKenna, with an address in Washington, D.C. Born a year before me. Probably about to graduate, unless he'd skipped a year somewhere, or was taking things slowly.

Hair: Brown. Eyes: Green. Height: 5'11". Weight: 174.

The picture matched. It was definitely him.

I handed it back. "Thanks."

"No problem." He put it back in his wallet, and the wallet back in his pocket, before nudging my room card, with the hotel logo prominently displayed. "This where you're staying?"

I nodded.

"Nice digs."

"Mackenzie is paying," I said, my tongue a little looser than usual from the drinks. Not that I was drunk or anything, just a little tipsy. "Quinn and I wouldn't be able to afford it on our own."

Going to Key West for spring break had been a last-minute decision. All the cheap places had been sold out. Quinn and I had talked about sharing, to cut costs, but Mackenzie had put her foot down on that idea. If we had any hope of getting laid, she told us, we needed separate rooms.

Ty peered into the corner again. "That's Mackenzie Forbes, isn't it?"

I nodded.

"You go to school with her?"

Yes, I did. Mackenzie had become a country music star at sixteen, and by the time eighteen rolled around, she was ready for some peace and quiet out of the public eye. So she'd enrolled at the University of Chicago, just like a normal person. We'd bonded in English 101 and been close ever since.

"She can afford it, I guess," Ty said.

Yes, she could. She'd just finished up her new album over Christmas break, and now she was in the process of finalizing her summer tour schedule. All she had to do to recoup the cost of Quinn's and my rooms, was sell a handful of extra tickets to one of her concerts.

That didn't mean I wasn't grateful, of course. She was going above and beyond the call of friendship. After all, she could have gone to Key West by herself. She didn't have to bring Quinn and me along.

"And I guess it makes sense that she'd want somewhere with good security," Ty added.

I hadn't thought about that, but yes. Sure. She'd told us stories about some of the more persistent of her fans, and I didn't blame her at all for wanting to feel safe. If someone was willing to break and enter to get his hands on my underwear, I'd want good security, too.

"D'you think maybe you should try to get in touch with your friend who left," Ty said, "and make sure she got there safely?"

Here we were, back to Quinn again. He seemed happy to talk about both my friends, but not so much interested in talking about me.

"What if she's with Ivy League Dude?" I said. Naked, in bed?

"Unless he's a total asshole," Ty answered, "he'll

understand."

"Even a nice guy might object to being disturbed under those circumstances."

But I fumbled for my phone anyway. It couldn't hurt to make sure. I hadn't been worried before—I wasn't really worried now—but Ty seemed so concerned about everyone's safety that I'd gotten a little concerned, too.

And besides, until I made sure, he probably wouldn't stop asking me to, so I may as well get it out of the way.

Usually we text each other—it's easier—but this time I actually dialed and waited for the phone to ring. If that didn't work, I'd try texting later. Although to be honest, Ty might not be satisfied until I'd actually heard Quinn's voice and made sure she was OK.

The phone rang twice, and then Quinn picked up. "Cassie?" She sounded worried. "Are you OK?"

"Fine," I said. "You?"

"Sure. Why?"

"Just checking. I met this guy—" I slanted a look at Ty across the bar; he grinned, "and he convinced me to call and make sure you got back to the hotel in one piece."

"Oh." There was a pause. I could tell she wanted to ask me more about the guy, but wasn't sure whether now was a good time. With him standing right next to me, I'd have to say it wasn't. "He must be pretty special," she said instead, "if he's checking up on your friends."

"Shut up." I glanced at Ty, guiltily. He winked. I made a half-turn away from him, in an attempt at a little more privacy. "So are you back at the hotel?"

"Just walked in," Quinn confirmed. "What about Mackenzie?"

"Found her hot musician with the tattoos and dumped me. Did you find someone to replace Ivy League Dude?"

"Yeah," Quinn said. "Ivy League Dude."

"He followed you?" I mean, obviously he had. I'd seen him go. But it seemed he'd also caught up to her and talked to her, not just done the weird, creepy, stalkery thing. *Good.*

"Yeah," Quinn said. "But he was OK."

I couldn't help but laugh. "Your tone says better than OK. I guess you forgave him, huh?"

"Guess so." I could tell she didn't really want to talk about it, and she wasted no time in changing the subject. "Go back to your really considerate hot guy. You know Mackenzie will never leave you alone if you don't get laid this trip."

Sure. I glanced at Ty and tried to imagine getting naked with him. It was surprisingly easy, if a little scary. "I'll catch up with you tomorrow," I told Quinn.

"Stay safe."

Oh, sure.

I dropped the phone into my bag and turned to Ty. "She's fine. Mostly sober, and back at the hotel. Alone." Or so I assumed. She hadn't sounded like she wasn't. Surely she wouldn't have told me I needed to get laid if she had Ivy League Dude with her?

Ty nodded. "What about you?"

"What about me?"

"Don't you think you should think about getting back to the hotel, too?"

"It's still early." Only ten thirty. "And I didn't come to Key West to sleep."

He smiled. "I'll go with you."

Oh, really? Well, that was a different matter, wasn't it?

I slid off the bar stool and onto the floor—it only heaved a little—and turned to catch Mackenzie's eye. She was wrapped up in her new guy, but not so much that she didn't see me standing there. I hooked my thumb toward the door. She nodded. And gave Ty a quick up and down and me a discreet thumbs up.

I grinned and turned back, and caught Ty grinning too. "That mean she approves?" he asked me.

I ducked my head so my hair covered my cheeks. "Seems that way."

"If we have Mackenzie's approval, let's get outta here." He nodded to the bartender as we headed for the exit. The bartender nodded back, busy swiping a wet rag over the bar.

"Friend of yours?" I asked, when we were outside in the street.

"I'm a friendly guy." He grinned, and then nodded to a cop hanging out just outside the door. "Evening, Officer."

The officer nodded back, and I could feel his eyes following us as we walked down the street.

There were plenty of cops out and about. Every block or so, we passed another. I had no idea why Ty was so worried. Key West during spring break looked like the safest place on earth.

He took the lead through the streets, and I hoped he knew where he was going, because I wasn't too sure. It was my first time in Key West, and with a glass of Sex on the Beach inside me, I wasn't thinking as clearly as maybe I should have been.

"I guess you've been here before?"

It looked like he hesitated before he answered. "Spring break last year. And a couple times with my parents growing up."

"It's my first time."

He slanted a look at me, lips curving. "No kidding?"

I flushed, and hoped the darkness hid it. "You know what I mean."

He laughed. "Sure." Another cop was standing on the corner, and he nodded again, before taking my arm to steer me across the street. "The hotel's just another block this way."

I nodded. "Are you studying criminal justice, or something?"

The fingers holding my arm tightened for a second, although his voice didn't change. "No, why?"

"You seem to like cops a lot. You're saying hi to all of them."

"Oh." He chuckled. "My dad's a cop. I've had respect for authority beaten into me."

"My dad's a minister."

He slanted me a look. "What's a nice girl like you doing in a dress like that?"

I'd thought my dress looked pretty good when I put it on, but suddenly I wasn't so sure. "It's Mackenzie's." Seeing as I didn't have anything so short or tight in my wardrobe.

"Then let Mackenzie wear it," Ty said. "And you dress like Cassie."

"Cassie doesn't know how to dress." Not to attract the attention of someone like him. He probably wouldn't have looked at me twice if it hadn't been for Mackenzie's hot pink, short, tight dress.

"Don't try to be somebody you're not. Who you are is fine." He stopped in front of the entrance to the hotel. "We're here."

We were, and sooner than I wanted to be. I glanced over my shoulder at the lighted lobby, and back at him. "You... um... you wanna come upstairs?"

Part of me hoped he'd say yes. The other part was terrified that he would.

He smiled. "I don't think I'd better."

"We wouldn't have to... I mean... we could just..."

The smile broadened. "Thanks, but I'd better get back. It was nice to meet you, Cassie."

"You too," I said.

"Maybe I'll see you around. Tomorrow."

"I'd like that."

I waited, but when he didn't make any kind of move, either toward me or away, I took a step closer and went up on my toes to kiss his cheek.

"Thank you for walking me home." Or not exactly home, but— "Here," I amended. "Thanks for walking me here."

He smelled good, like soap and fresh air. "You're welcome. I was happy to do it."

"Are you sure you won't change your mind?" I nodded to the door.

"Maybe some other time. When you're sober."

"I'm not drunk." A little tipsy, maybe. But just a little.

He smiled. “I didn’t say you were. But when I take a girl to bed, I like her to remember me the next morning.”

“I’d remember you,” I said.

“Good. Then I’ll see you later.” He winked, and this time he did walk away.

I stood there for a second and watched, just in case he changed his mind. But although he did look over his shoulder once, it was only to point to the door to the hotel. I sighed and went inside.

Foiled again.

CHAPTER *Two*

Since I'd gone to bed early and alone, I had no problem waking up with the sun the next morning. Or if not exactly with the sun, it was fairly early by the time I made my way out of the hotel for a walk on the beach.

I'd snagged a croissant from the continental breakfast bar on my way past, and was munching as I walked. Where the beach met the street, I stopped to kick off my shoes and walk barefoot in the sand.

I'd told Ty the truth about where I'd grown up. A small town in the middle of Ohio, surrounded by cornfields and cows. Dirt, earth, and grass. As landlocked as it's possible to get.

Now that I lived in Chicago, I couldn't get enough of the lake. It was gorgeous, and looked sort of like the ocean.

Until I came to Key West. The knowledge that this really was the ocean, that if I started swimming, the next thing I'd reach was Cuba, was mind-blowing.

You're not in Kansas anymore, Cassie.

Or Ohio. Or even Chicago.

It was beautiful. Beyond beautiful. Breathtaking. The beach was white, the water a clear azure blue. The lake was pretty, but not pretty like this.

And I had it almost to myself. The streets had been deserted when I walked through town. Key West was definitely a vacation-town: people stayed up half the night and slept in. Most of the businesses were still closed—with the exception of the hotels and coffee shops—and the few people I'd seen had been dragging themselves home, still thinking it was yesterday. Today wouldn't be starting for them until they'd had some sleep.

The beach had only a few people on it. An older couple strolled hand in hand in the surf. A woman jogged with a small dog on a leash. What looked like a homeless man was curled up in sleep, bearded and scruffy. This was probably paradise for people like him. It never got cold and rarely got uncomfortable here.

There were no homeless in Braxton. Everyone in town knows everyone else, and no one would let that happen to any of us.

There were a lot of homeless in Chicago, and I always felt bad when I saw them huddled on the corners in the snow.

I gave the man a wide berth and kept going. Next up were a couple of college kids, probably not homeless, but also sleeping on the beach. Wrapped in each other's arms, like Romeo and Juliet. The girl had her head on the guy's shoulder, and his arm lay across her waist. She had long, shiny, dark hair that spread across his chest and her face, and for a second I thought it was Quinn, but it wasn't.

Of course not. Quinn had spent the night in the hotel.

There were footsteps behind me, and then a voice. "Everything OK?"

I turned and smiled at Ty. "Seems to be."

"Someone you know?" He was hardly breathless at all, even though his chest was glistening with sweat. His very, very bare chest.

Whoa. Nice six-pack under that fake FBI shirt he wasn't wearing.

"Um..." I said, scrambling to remember what it was he'd asked before I got bowled over by the visuals. *Oh, right.* "No. At first it looked a little like Quinn. Same hair. But it isn't."

He peered past me. "They look all right. We should probably just let 'em sleep."

I nodded. I hadn't thought to do anything different.

Now that we'd established that everything was fine, I figured he'd probably take off running again, but when I started walking, he fell into step beside me. "How's it going?"

"Fine," I said.

"Headache?"

I shook my head. "I told you. I wasn't drunk."

He nodded. "You're up early."

"So are you."

He grinned. "I wasn't drunk either."

I hadn't thought he was.

We walked a few steps in silence. Until he glanced at me. "So tell me, what's a nice girl—a preacher's kid, no less—doing in Key West for spring break?"

"Whatever she wants," I said, and got a smile for my trouble.

I basked in it for a moment before I continued. "I told you. Mackenzie wanted to come. Spring break is kind of part of the whole college experience."

He didn't say anything, and I added, "It's like she's two different people, you know? America's Sweetheart—the one everybody knows about, and when she goes out with a new guy, his face is all over the internet the next day. But the rest of the time she's just plain Mackenzie Forbes. The one who wants a normal life without everyone watching her every move."

He nodded. "But that's Mackenzie. What made Cassie decide to come to Key West?"

"Other than that Mackenzie asked me and Quinn to go

with her? I guess it's the same reason, really. Just different."

He looked confused, and I tried to explain. "I grew up in a small town. The kind where everybody knows everybody else. You couldn't step a toe over the line without somebody noticing."

Mackenzie has the whole world watching her. I only had all of Braxton. But it was still frustrating.

"Yeah," Ty said, "but you're in Chicago now. And probably have been for a couple of years, right?"

Right. But campus was really just like a small town, and somehow I seemed to have taken my reputation with me. Somehow, word had gotten around.

Stay away from Cassie Wilder, her dad's a preacher.

Stay away from Cassie Wilder, she's still a virgin.

The word might as well be tattooed across my forehead in big, red letters, the way all the guys I'd met in Chicago had steered clear of me. You'd think someone might be interested in being a girl's first, but no. At the rate I was going, I'd graduate a virgin.

Hell, at the rate I was going, I'd probably die one.

But of course I couldn't tell Ty any of that. If he knew, he wouldn't want to talk to me anymore, either.

So I settled for a slightly more general version of the truth.

"I guess I thought Key West might be somewhere where I could be someone else for a while." Someone more exciting and less virginal. Less 'nice.' Hence the short and tight dress he'd commented on yesterday. And hence the glass of Sex on the Beach I'd managed to choke down before I gave up and ordered Sprite instead.

With a wedge of lime, so I wouldn't look like the loser I was.

"I think you're probably fine the way you are," Ty said.

"Thank you." Although I obviously wasn't fine enough for him to want anything to do with.

By now we were nearing the end of the beach, marked by a big pile of stones reaching out into the ocean. I had my mouth open to suggest that maybe we needed to turn back, when Ty stopped. "Shit."

"What?"

He glanced at me. "Stay here."

"What? Why?"

But by then I'd seen what he'd seen. "Oh, my God. Is she alive?"

He didn't tell me again to stay where I was. And when I followed him up the beach to the girl sprawled there, he didn't tell me not to.

She was my age, or maybe a year or two younger. A freshman or sophomore? So pale her skin was almost the same color as the sand, and with light hair, as well. If it hadn't been for the splotch of pink fabric a few feet away, I'm not sure we would have noticed her.

She was naked except for a pair of hoop earrings. A bra lay a few feet away, virginal white, and farther on, what looked like a dress, similar to the one I'd worn last night. Bright and tight. That's what I'd noticed, and probably Ty too. A pair of flip-flops was scattered, one in one direction, one in the other.

There were bruises on her thighs, I saw, and a trickle of something dark—maybe blood? And that's as much as I had time for, because Ty turned to me, his voice tight. "Got your phone on you?"

I blinked at him, stupidly, before the words registered. "Yes."

"Call 9-1-1. Tell them we need an ambulance and the cops."

He turned back to the girl without waiting for my answer.

I fumbled my phone out of the pocket of my shorts, my hands shaking. "Is she alive?" She must be, right? If he thought an ambulance could do her any good?

He nodded, on his knees next to her. "Just unconscious."

"Oh. Good." I managed to punch in the right numbers and hold the phone to my ear. When the dispatcher came on, I even managed to relay the information, though my teeth were chattering. "They'll be here in ten minutes," I told Ty when I'd hung up, my voice shaking.

His brows lowered. "They didn't tell you to stay on the phone?"

I shook my head.

"They're supposed to do that."

"Maybe they only have one phone line. Maybe she needed it to call the ambulance and the police."

He shrugged and turned back to the girl on the sand. I took a careful step closer—but not too close. I felt guilty, like I should be doing something, but I didn't know what, and besides, she was so very... naked. It seemed wrong to be staring at her, but at the same time, it was impossible not to.

I looked out toward the ocean and then back. "Shouldn't we... do something?"

"We are doing something," Ty said. "We've called the cops."

"I mean for her. CPR or something?"

He shook his head. "She doesn't need help breathing. She's alive. She's just not waking up." There was a trace of something, almost like anger, in his voice. Or maybe it was frustration. That made more sense.

I twined my fingers together. "What do you think happened?"

"Isn't it obvious?" He glanced up at me, his eyes as hard and cold as emeralds. "She went out drinking, picked up the wrong guy, and got raped."

Oh, God. What little color was left in my cheeks drained out. I'd suspected it, of course—like he said, it was obvious—but it was different to hear him say it. I swallowed. "Are you sure?"

My voice came out in a whisper.

He looked at me, probably about to say something scathing—but then he didn't. Instead he closed his eyes for a second and took a breath. And another. When he opened them again, they were back to normal. So was his voice. "No. I'm not sure. I'm guessing. She's naked, on the beach, and she looks like she's had rough sex. Somebody was with her last night. Somebody who left her here. But I don't know that she was raped."

I nodded. That was a slight improvement, even if he'd only said it to make me feel better.

It felt like an eternity before the ambulance and police cars arrived, but in reality, it wasn't even ten minutes. More like seven or eight.

They drove right up on the beach, and over to where we were. Two police cars and one ambulance. The police cars had suns peeping out from behind the P in Police, and their slogan was *Protecting and Serving Paradise.*

A couple of officers in uniform began stringing crime scene tape around the area with the body. Another guy in regular clothes came out of the second car, while two paramedics hopped down from the ambulance and dragged a gurney out of the back.

Ty got to his feet and stepped up next to me.

The plain-clothes cop stalked up to us. "You the ones who called it in?"

Ty glanced at me. I nodded.

"Ricky Fuentes, Key West PD." He flashed a badge. Unnecessary, when I'd just seen him come out of a police car, but maybe he had to. Procedure. "You wanna tell me what happened?"

His voice had just a trace of a Spanish accent, and he had big, dark eyes, and golden skin. He was no taller than Ty, but somehow he seemed to tower over both of us. I swallowed.

"I was running," Ty said evenly. "Cassie was walking. We got down here and saw her."

Fuentes looked at me. "Name?"

I cleared my throat. "Cassandra Wilder."

"How long are you in town for, Cassandra?"

"We came on Saturday," I said, wishing my voice was as even as Ty's. It wasn't. I sounded like a thirteen-year-old boy.

Squeaky. "We're leaving again next Saturday. Spring break."

"Going back to?"

"University of Chicago."

He nodded.

"I'm Ty McKenna," Ty added. "Washington, D.C. Georgetown University."

Fuentes looked momentarily taken aback at the unsolicited introduction, but then he rallied. "Either of you know this girl?"

All three of us turned to look at her, but in my case at least, it wasn't because I needed to see her again. I knew very well that I didn't know her. "I've never seen her before."

"You?" Fuentes asked Ty.

He shrugged. "I think I may have seen her yesterday."

I turned to him. "Really?"

"In the bar. There was a girl there with blond hair and a pink dress."

"I was wearing a pink dress," I pointed out, although I doubted he needed the refresher.

He glanced at me. "Not you. Another girl."

"Are you sure it's her?"

"No," Ty said. "She was conscious and dressed then. Walking and talking. It's a little hard to tell. But it could have been."

"Which bar was this?" Fuentes had a little notebook out, with a pencil stub ready to go.

"Captain Crow's," Ty said, "on Duval."

Fuentes jotted it down. "That where you two met?"

I glanced at Ty. He glanced back. "Yes. Last night."

Fuentes smirked. "And then you got up this morning and decided to take a walk on the beach?"

I flushed at the implication. Ty didn't react, of course. "We didn't spend the night together."

Fuentes's eyebrows moved. "That so?"

"Yes," I said. "He walked me to my hotel and left."

"Where are you staying, Ms. Wilder?"

I told him the name of the hotel, and he wrote it down. "So you decided on your own to take a walk on the beach."

It sounded like an accusation. I flushed. "The weather was pretty. I was awake."

"The weather's always pretty," Fuentes said. "Did you see anyone while you were walking?"

"Lots of people. Ty." I glanced at him. "A lady with a dog. An old couple walking. A young couple sleeping. And a homeless guy, also sleeping."

He turned to Ty, who added a few more sightings to the list. He must have run farther than I had walked, and seen more people.

"I don't suppose..."

The both turned to look at me, and I dug my teeth into my bottom lip.

"What?" Ty said.

"The homeless guy. You don't think he...?"

"We'll find out." Fuentes's voice had a distinct note of don't-tell-me-how-to-do-my-job. "What did you do after you dropped her off last night?" he asked Ty.

If Ty was bothered by the question, or the tone of voice, he didn't show it. "Went back to Captain Crow's for another beer. Then home."

"To your hotel?"

Ty nodded.

"And where's that?"

Ty rattled off the information, while I was hung up on that 'other' beer.

If he'd had a first beer, I hadn't noticed. He hadn't had anything in his hand when I saw him. Although he might have been between drinks right then, I suppose.

"Can anyone verify when you came in?" Fuentes asked, shocking me off my train of thought.

"Why does he need someone to verify it?"

They both turned to me. "Someone did something to this girl," Ty said after a beat, when it became obvious that Fuentes wasn't going to speak first. "The detective is making sure I have an alibi."

"If you did this, why would you come back here this morning? Wouldn't it make more sense to stay away?"

"Maybe I'm trying to make sure any DNA they find can be explained away."

Fuentes arched his brows.

"His dad's a cop," I said.

Fuentes glanced at Ty. "Is that so?"

Ty shrugged. "I don't know if anyone saw me come in last night. It isn't the kind of place where you have to go through the lobby to the rooms. I guess you'll have to check."

"Don't worry," Fuentes said, closing his notebook with a little flap of pages, and shoving it in his pocket, "we'll do that."

There was a pause. While we'd been talking, the paramedics had lifted the girl onto the gurney and covered her with a sheet up to her chin. One of the cops was watching, while the other was walking around the crime scene dropping little markers here and there on the sand where he'd found something of interest. One by the bra, one by each shoe, one by the dress.

"Gotta wallet over here, Detective!" he called.

Fuentes lifted a finger and turned back to us. "You two can go. If I have any more questions, I know where to find you."

I nodded. Ty hesitated, but after a second he nodded too.

"Are you OK?" I asked when we were outside the area roped off by the cops and well away from the action, where no one could hear us.

He glanced at me. "I guess. As OK as I have a right to be."

Well, obviously. We were neither of us totally OK. But we were a lot more OK than the girl back there, who still hadn't woken up.

"Why is she still unconscious, do you think?"

Ty shrugged. "Trauma? Her body shut down so her mind won't have to deal with what happened? Or maybe someone gave her something. Spiked her drink or whatever."

I shivered, in spite of the tropical heat. "This is scary. That's why you took my glass away last night, isn't it? Someone could have put something in it."

"The thought crossed my mind."

We walked a few steps in silence.

"Thank you," I said. "If it hadn't been for you, that could have been me, back there."

"We don't know that," Ty answered. "But be careful from now on, OK?"

Oh, yes. I intended to be very, very careful. And tell both my friends to be, as well.

CHAPTER *Three*

He walked me back to the hotel again, and just like last night, stopped outside the front entrance. "Home, sweet home."

"Thank you," I said. "Again."

"You're welcome. Again."

We stood for a second and looked at each other. I tried my very best not to let my eyes stray below his chin, but it wasn't easy. He wasn't glistening anymore, but that six-pack was still there and very much on display.

"What kind of sport do you do?"

He grinned and I blushed. He probably knew exactly why I'd asked, because he'd guessed exactly what I was thinking. God, what I wouldn't give for just a little of Quinn's sophistication.

He took pity on me. "None, really. I run and lift weights, but I haven't played a sport since—"

He stopped.

"Since—?"

He looked at me again. "High school. I did track and field in high school."

"Georgetown has a track and field team, don't they?"

"Yeah. I'm just... busy."

OK, then. "You probably want to get back to your own place and take a shower."

"I wouldn't mind," Ty said.

"I'd offer you the use of mine—" preferably after a round of mind-blowing devirginization, "but I assume you'll just say no."

He smiled. "You gotta be careful who you say stuff like that to, Cassie. Someone else might take you up on it."

I didn't want anyone else to take me up on it. I wanted *him*. So I wasn't about to extend the invitation to anyone else. And I wasn't sure how I felt about the fact that he seemed to think I would. "I'm not promiscuous, you know. I just... like you."

"Thank you. I like you too."

But not enough to sleep with me.

I didn't say it, though. Just wished him a good day and headed upstairs to shower and change into my bikini, so I could spend some quality time by the pool, working on my tan. It seemed a nice, safe place to be, surrounded by people; a place where I could keep my drink in sight the whole time I was there, to make sure no one had a chance to tamper with it.

The morning passed slowly and lazily. I read, I dozed, and I admired the view. There was some prime USDA beef on display, and some of it did its best to attract attention. I've never seen so many muscles flexing.

A little after noon, the guy Mackenzie had been making out with last night showed up. He was alone, though, so either they hadn't spent the night together, or they were trying to make it look like they hadn't. I glanced around for Mackenzie, but she wasn't there.

Mr. Tat peeled his T-shirt off and dropped it on an empty chaise. Then he made himself comfortable on the chaise next to it and put on a pair of sunglasses. He leaned back and acted like he was soaking up the sun, although he looked a whole lot less relaxed than I got the feeling he was trying to look like he was. I know his eyes weren't closed, because when a couple girls stopped in front of him, the glasses came off before they spoke. He'd obviously been watching from behind the lenses.

The girls were pretty, but it was clear from his body language that he wasn't interested. They did their best, but Mr. Tat shook his head. The girls tried again, cocking their hips and sticking their chests out. He kept shaking his head. Eventually they acknowledged defeat and slunk off, pouting. Mr. Tat leaned back and tried to make himself look relaxed again.

And then the door to the hotel opened and Mackenzie came out, and I saw him stiffen like a pointer.

He tried not to let it show, like he wasn't watching every step she took toward him, but he was painfully obvious. I just hoped Mackenzie could see it.

He whisked the shirt off the empty chaise and she sat down. And after that I stopped watching, because it felt a little pervy to be staring at my best friend working on getting laid.

She liked him, I could tell. I just hoped he liked her for her, and not because she was Mackenzie Forbes, rich and famous.

It didn't take them long to leave. I stayed by the pool, under an umbrella during the hottest part of the day. Quinn never showed up. I thought about calling her again to make sure she was OK, especially after what had happened this morning, but then I thought she might not appreciate it, so I didn't.

Horrible, though, what had happened to that girl. Or what I assumed had happened to her, anyway. I didn't really know the details, and I didn't think I wanted to.

But also horrible to think it might have been me if Ty hadn't taken my glass away last night.

I shivered in spite of the heat and sun. I wanted to get rid of my virginity, but I didn't want to get rid of it that way.

The girl on the beach had had what looked like dried blood between her legs. Did that mean she'd been a virgin?

Had whoever raped her known that?

I suppressed another chill and glanced around. Time to go inside. I felt exposed out here. I knew I was just imagining things, but I felt like people were staring at me.

That guy on the other side of the pool, the jock in the red trunks with the crew cut... surely he was looking at me like he'd like to do something to me. Wasn't he?

And the one in the pool, bobbing near my end... was he over here so he could look at me and fantasize about leaving me sprawled unconscious on the beach tomorrow morning?

I gathered my stuff and fled.

I put on jeans and a T-shirt to go out that night. No more short, clingy dresses for me. And no crazy heels. I made sure my shoes were sensible, because the last thing I wanted was to find myself in a situation I couldn't run away from. Call it preventative measures. I know that wearing revealing clothes doesn't mean you're asking for it, but there was no sense in being stupid, either.

Both Mackenzie and Quinn were still MIA. Mackenzie was with Mr. Tat, probably. They'd looked pretty chummy when they left the pool in the afternoon. By now they'd probably had hot, sweaty sex at least twice, and were planning to go for broke. Or maybe they'd gone somewhere for dinner and to refuel. Or were having dinner in bed, courtesy of room service.

I had no idea where Quinn was. I hadn't seen her since last night. But she seemed to be doing all right. I'd sent her a text asking if she wanted to come out with me, and had gotten a 'thanks but no thanks,' back. *Not now. Busy.*

All righty, then.

I could have stuck around the hotel, I guess, and not ventured out into the town. It would have been safer, and perfectly acceptable. There were a couple of bars on the first and second levels, and they were hopping. But—I admit it—I was hoping to see Ty again, and Ty had been at Captain Crow's on Duval.

So in the direction of Captain Crow's on Duval I went.

It was a perfect evening for walking around. The temperature hovered around seventy degrees. Average high for Chicago this time of year was mid-forties, so Key West was a lot nicer. I could feel the air cool against my arms, but not in an uncomfortable way. And the knowledge that at home I'd be wearing a coat, went a long way toward making me feel better.

There were plenty of people out, and like last night, there were a lot of cops. Practically every block had a cop on it. It was hard to believe the Key West police force had so many officers, so maybe they'd called in the reserves for spring break. They probably had, because things were kind of crazy. Some people must have been drinking since they got up this morning, and they were staggering around squealing and giggling and cursing.

On a corner halfway to the bar, outside the Old Town cemetery, I saw one of the cops from this morning. At least I was pretty sure it was him. He must be pulling a double shift.

I slowed down and smiled. "Hi."

He nodded.

"You were at the beach this morning, right?"

He hesitated, and in the silence I could hear the murmur of voices. He must have heard them too, because his eyes flickered left and right.

I'd wanted to ask about the girl, whether she'd woken up and said anything about what happened to her, but if he wasn't even going to admit to having been there, I didn't think he'd volunteer any information.

And then two people came out of the cemetery, and the opportunity passed. I trudged on, looking around.

Key West is a pretty interesting place, in a creepy, romantic sort of way.

Originally, it was called Bone Island, or Bone Key: Cayo Hueso in Spanish. After that, it was named Thompson's Island for a while, after the Secretary of the Navy, but obviously that name didn't stick. And then there are some who think it's called Key West because it's the westernmost of the Florida Keys.

Several presidents have spent time in Key West, and Harry Truman had his Winter White House here. After Truman left office, the house became the place where the presidents dealt with the Cold War, because of Key West's proximity to Cuba. Truman's Winter White House is a museum now; a big white house on Front Street, surrounded by palm trees.

Not too far from there is the house where Ernest Hemingway wrote *To Have and Have Not* back in the 1930s. That's a museum now, as well. I should probably go check it out while I was here.

Sure, going to museums wasn't what Mackenzie had planned for us when we came to Key West to relax and have fun, but after two days of sitting around doing nothing, I was beginning to get bored, to be honest. It was OK for Mackenzie: she'd found a guy to spend time with. And obviously Quinn had figured something out too. I was the only one at loose ends.

Unless you can convince Ty to keep you company.

Yeah. Because he'd been beating down my door so far.

Anyway, surely a museum would be safe? Nobody was likely to spike my drink in a museum.

So, decision made. Unless something good happened tonight—unless Ty decided to stop playing hard to get and decided to do something to relieve me of my virginity—I was going sightseeing tomorrow.

Halfway down the next block, a small group of tourists were gathered for what looked like a ghost tour, with a guide in nineteenth-century costume, with a tall, black hat and a white face. When I slowed down in passing, he smiled invitingly. "Care to join us?"

I hesitated. "I don't know. How long is the tour?"

"The trolley tour is about two and a half hours. But we have walking tours, too."

"But this is the trolley tour?"

He nodded, gesturing to a trolley rolling silently down the street toward us. It was black, with the name of the tour company in florescent letters on the side. And it wasn't really a trolley—no tracks—just a bus or van of some kind made up to look like a trolley. As it came closer, I could see the pictures of ghostly apparitions decorating the front and sides. White ladies with flowing hair, pirates with eyepatches, evil-looking children.

"I'm not sure," I said.

He grinned, wide enough to show canine teeth. "Scared?"

Not really scared. More afraid that I'd miss Ty, that he'd go to Captain Crow's and then leave again—maybe with someone else—because I wasn't there.

I took a step back. "Maybe tomorrow night. I don't have enough time now."

He nodded. "Hang on a sec."

The trolley rolled up to the curb next to us and the tourists began climbing onboard. The driver was another dude in old clothes, with his hair in ringlets and Jack Sparrow eye makeup, I guess to make it look like his eye sockets were empty.

"Lucky thirteen," the guy on the sidewalk told him.

I did a quick headcount as the tourist filed onboard, and yes, there were thirteen of them.

As the trolley pulled away from the curb, the driver began speaking. He must have a microphone clipped to his costume, because his voice was magnified enough that I could hear him as he drove down the street. "Good evening, ladies and gentleman. My name is Augustus G. Loomis, captain of the *Gulf Stream Phantom*—"

I turned to the guy who had stayed behind. "Augustus Loomis?"

His voice took on the cadences of a storyteller, all deep and mysterious. "A wrecker in old Key West. His ship, the *Gulf Stream Phantom*, ran aground near the Dry Tortugas in November of 1859. A few days later, old Augustus's body washed up on the southern shore of Key West. It's said he's still haunting the Isle of Bones, scanning the horizon for any sign of his missing ship or crew."

Yikes.

I cleared my throat. "Um... I have heard that Key West is called the Isle of Bones, but I don't know why."

"Ah." He smiled. "It's because of the bones, lass."

Lass? Were we Scottish now? "What bones?"

"The bones that were littered all over the ground when the settlers arrived."

I blinked. "Where did they all come from?"

The guy shrugged. "Who knows? Pirates? Native Americans? Voodoo?"

"And... um... who are you supposed to be?"

He whipped off his hat and bowed. "Talbott Jehosephat Windsor, at your service."

"Nice to meet you." *Not*. "Um... who was Talbott Jehosephat Windsor?"

"*I*," Mr. Windsor said, with emphasis, "drove a hearse for a local funerary establishment during the yellow fever epidemic in the late 1800s. When I died, my bone cart was displayed in the East Martello Fort, now a museum. I haunt the place looking for it."

Ah. "That's... interesting."

He smiled, going back to normal. Or whatever passed for normal around here. "We're all real people."

Right. Too bad I wasn't sure whether the real people he was referring to were the dead ones, or the ones he and the others had been born as.

"Do you have a brochure? Maybe I can come back tomorrow."

He dug one out of his pocket. I folded it up small and stuck it in mine. "Thank you."

He nodded. "Be careful tonight, lass. There's evil in the air. I can smell it."

His nostrils flared as if he actually could. I don't think it's possible to smell evil—unless it smells like sulfur, the way my dad says—but I smiled politely. "I'll do that."

By the time I got to the corner and turned around, he was still standing there staring after me.

Captain Crow's was hopping, just like the night before. I had to go sideways through the door to get inside and over to the bar.

The same bartender was on duty as yesterday, and I ordered a Sprite while I looked around for anyone I knew.

There was no sign of Quinn, not that I had expected there to be. This really wasn't her kind of scene, any more than it was mine. Or Mackenzie's, for that matter, for all that she tried to pretend to be comfortable with it.

Anyway, Ivy League Dude was missing too. He was a good-looking guy, with dark, curly hair and blue eyes, and if he'd been there, I think I would have noticed. So maybe he and Quinn were together.

It just figured, didn't it? Everyone was getting lucky but me.

I had a quick glance around for Ty, but didn't see him.

Ivy League Dude's friends were here, though. Four or five of them, at a table by the wall. They were doing shots of Tequila again, and judging from the way they hooted and hollered, they'd already had a few.

I tilted my head and contemplated them. Good-looking guys. Well-dressed. Obviously wealthy. Expensive haircuts. Even their casual clothes had brand name logos. Money no object. They were probably used to getting whatever they wanted.

If one of them wanted a girl and she said no, was he the kind of guy who'd rape her and leave her unconscious on the beach?

Nasty thought, but... maybe. If he was used to skating. If he was used to Daddy's money getting him out of whatever scrapes he got himself into.

Then yes, maybe.

The bartender put my glass of Sprite in front of me, and jerked me back to reality.

"Thanks," I said, dipping my fingers into my pocket for money to pay him. No purse for me tonight. I'd stuffed everything in my pockets. "Have you seen Ty?"

His eyes turned flat. "Who?"

"The guy I was talking to yesterday. Sort of dark blond, light brown hair. Wore a blue T-shirt with an FBI logo on it."

"There were a lot of people in here yesterday," the bartender said and walked off.

Huh. I put the money I owed him on the bar and swiveled the stool to further survey the room.

Was Ty right that the girl on the beach had been here last night?

A blonde in a pink dress.

I'd been a blonde in a pink dress yesterday. I tried to remember whether I'd seen another, but I couldn't. If I'd come face to face with a replica of myself, it hadn't registered.

Then again, I hadn't been here all night. It depended on when Ty had seen her. And she probably hadn't been an exact replica. When I saw her this morning, it hadn't struck me that we looked alike.

The girl on the sand had had very fair hair, almost platinum blond. Mine was darker, more like dishwater. And mine was shorter, only shoulder length. Hers had looked like it would come halfway down her back. And the hot pink dress on the sand had been a different shade than the one I'd been wearing, as well.

Still, 'a blonde in a pink dress' could apply to both of us.

I took a sip of the Sprite and wondered whether that meant anything. Did someone have a particular thing for blondes in pink dresses? Or a grudge against them?

If so, I ought to be safe tonight. I was wearing jeans and a white T-shirt. And my drink tasted normal. The bartender had poured it for me himself, and it hadn't left my hand since.

Although as far as doping drinks went, who'd have better

opportunity than the bartender?

I glanced at him, moving around behind the bar, doing bartendery things. Did he seem like the kind of nutcase who would drug and rape girls?

He was in his mid-thirties, or maybe closer to forty, and looked fairly normal. Not like he'd be dangerous at all. He was wearing jeans and a T-shirt with the name of the bar on the back, and he had a goatee and a tattoo of Celtic knots around his wrist. I'd certainly seen scarier people. Talbott Jehosephat Windsor, just to name one.

Then again, it's usually the ones who don't look dangerous that are, isn't it? Unless you're stupid, you avoid the ones who look like they could hurt you. It's the ones who look harmless but aren't that you have to watch out for.

A movement in the corner of the room caught my eye, and I glanced in that direction. And felt my stomach drop onto the floor.

There he was. Ty.

And he wasn't alone.

CHAPTER *Four*

It was ridiculous that that should bother me. I'd met the guy all of twice. He'd turned me down both times. He'd even been nice about it. He clearly wasn't interested, or if he was, he wasn't interested in doing anything about it. The fact that he was here with another girl shouldn't bother me.

It did.

A lot.

And she wasn't just any girl, either. If he'd gone out looking for someone who was the opposite of me in every way, he couldn't have done a better job.

This girl had everything I didn't, and I don't just mean Ty. Long, dark hair. A fabulous tan. Fat lips. Legs up to her armpits. The kind of body that didn't quit. And if she had anything stamped across her forehead, it sure wasn't 'virgin.' In fact, her tank top—short, tight, low cut, stretched to bursting point across a pair of honeydew-sized breasts—said it all.

Save a virgin. Do me instead.

My face twisted. This was what Ty wanted?

It was no wonder he'd turned me down, was it? I couldn't hope to compete.

But on the other hand, did I really want to?

I mean, she might have Ty, but would I trade a couple of days with him for all my dignity?

Um... no. I actually wouldn't. It would be a cold day in hell before I put on a T-shirt that said something that stupid. I could just imagine the expression on my mother's and father's faces if I'd come home wearing something like it.

So yeah, if she was what Ty wanted—if he'd really rather have that tramp than me—then that was his loss and not mine. He obviously wasn't worth my time and effort.

But no matter how much I justified it, I couldn't keep my stomach from twisting as I watched her stick her chest practically in his face and bat her eyelashes at him. Fake. They had to be. Nobody's been blessed with assets like those.

And I'm not just talking about the eyelashes here.

And to add insult to injury, he was smiling down at her like he enjoyed the display.

He even winked.

I swiveled around on my chair again and put my back to them. My face in the mirror behind the bar looked like I'd bit into a lemon.

"Here, sugar." The bartender slid another glass in front of me. From the looks of it, it was more Sprite. Clear and bubbly. "On the house."

I couldn't quite tell whether his tone was sympathetic or malicious, or maybe a mixture of both.

"Thanks." I pulled it closer, but didn't drink. No sense in letting disappointment make me stupid, after all.

After a moment, he grabbed my empty glass and walked off. I left the new glass on the counter and slid off the stool.

I was almost to the door when Ty looked up and spotted me.

And worse than that, didn't just spot me, but spotted me looking at him.

Because, idiot that I was, I just couldn't not look at him one last time before I walked out.

And when I saw that he'd seen me, I didn't look away and walk out the door.

No, I looked back at him, caught and held by those incredibly green eyes. I'm sure he could see exactly how upset I was. Even if I'd tried my best to tell myself I didn't care.

And then, like an idiot, I stood there, staring stupidly at him. He was the one who looked away first, back to Ms. Do Me.

And that's when I turned around and went out the door.

I hadn't gone more than half a block before I heard footsteps behind me. "Cassie!"

I didn't have to look over my shoulder. I recognized the voice. I pumped my arms and walked faster.

"Cassie! Wait up!"

"I don't want to talk to you," I said, when he come up on the side of me. "Go back to what's-her-name."

He fell into step next to me and stuffed his hands in his pockets. "Charisma. Her name is Charisma."

Of course it was. I snorted.

"Or at least that's what she told me." He was smiling, I could hear it in his voice. "She's a drama major at Syracuse. I think it's her stage name."

No kidding. "She's a bit obvious," I said, "don't you think?"

And not just in giving herself pseudonyms.

Speaking of T-shirts—not that I had been—Ty's was white today. With black letters. *I don't need sex. The government fucks me every day.*

I wondered how his dad, the cop—presumably a government employee—felt about that. The same way my parents would have felt about Charisma's *Save a Virgin* shirt, probably.

"It isn't what you think," he told me.

"What isn't?"

I knew I shouldn't be talking to him. I should tell him to get lost and go back to the hotel by myself. He'd looked much too chummy with Charisma—or whatever her real name was. Hopefully something like Gladys. Or Edna. Maybe even Hortense.

But I couldn't. Now that he was here, walking next to me, smiling at me with those green eyes and that dimple... I didn't have it in me to tell him to leave me alone.

I could hear Mackenzie's voice in my head. *You have it bad, Cass.*

Yes, I did. And for a guy who obviously didn't care whether I lived or died.

Although actually, that wasn't true. He cared enough that he'd walked me home last night. And this morning.

He cared enough that he was walking me home now, too. Enough that he'd left Charisma when he saw me.

Maybe it would be OK to be a little bit encouraged by that. Even if he didn't want to sleep with me.

"She's down here with a couple of friends," Ty continued. "One of them was the girl we found on the beach this morning."

That got my attention, anyway.

I turned to him, my eyes wide. "How do you know?"

He hesitated a second. "I realized I'd seen her before. Last night."

"You said that this morning. To Detective Fuentes."

"Charisma," Ty said. "I realized I'd seen Charisma before. Last night. And I thought that the blonde in the pink dress was with her."

"And was she?"

He nodded. "Her name's Elizabeth."

"Another drama student?"

"English Lit," Ty said.

Like me. Great.

"I don't suppose you know whether she's woken up and told anyone anything? Like, who did it?"

He shook his head. "Charisma said Elizabeth doesn't

remember anything. She was in the bar last night, and she woke up in the hospital this morning. And that's it. She doesn't remember anything that happened in between."

"Drugs, then."

He nodded. "Watch what you put in your mouth."

I shot him a look. But the double entendre didn't seem to have occurred to him, and since we were talking about something fairly serious, it was probably better not to point it out.

"I already am," I said.

"Tell your friends, too. Don't leave drinks unattended. Don't accept drinks from strangers."

"Like the drink you offered to buy me last night?"

He grinned. "Yeah. Like that one. Although if you think back, you may remember I didn't actually get you one."

No, he hadn't. "The bartender gave me a Sprite on the house," I confessed. "Just now. I was too worried to drink it."

He smiled. "I think anything Barry gives you is probably OK. He's been running Captain Crow's for years."

Maybe so. Then again— "If the girl—Elizabeth—was doped there, it doesn't hurt to be careful."

"No," Ty agreed, his dimple disappearing, "it doesn't."

We walked a few yards in silence. Just like yesterday—just like when I came this way thirty or forty minutes ago—the streets were full of people. Students on spring break, a few other tourist types, locals taking advantage of the hoopla, and cops.

"I'm going sightseeing tomorrow," I told Ty.

He glanced at me. "Yeah?"

"I'm tired of sitting by the pool and working on my tan. So I'm going to see the Hemingway House and the Little Truman House and the state park with the fort, and maybe take a ghost tour."

He smiled again. "Those are fun."

"Have you been on one?"

He shook his head. "Not here. But I come from the

Jacksonville area. St. Augustine is there, and it's the oldest city in the U.S. It's full of ghosts, and it has great ghost tours."

"I've never been to St. Augustine," I admitted.

"You should go sometime. It's like this, but not so crazy. No nightlife to speak of. Just a lot of history and really nice beaches."

"That sounds nice." What would be even nicer was if he offered to show me around his hometown sometime.

He didn't, though. I added, "You're welcome to come on the tour with me tomorrow. If you don't have plans. We can hunt for ghosts together."

"Oh." He looked surprised, and then guilty. "I'm not sure..."

"It's OK. Forget I asked."

We walked forward in silence.

"Tell you what," Ty said, "if you have twenty minutes, we can hunt for ghosts together right now."

I squinted at him, not entirely sure what he was getting at.

"The old Key West Cemetery is just a block away. It's full of dead people."

"Is it haunted?"

Ty shrugged. "We can walk through and see. It won't take long. It's practically on the way."

I hesitated, and he winked at me. "I'll hold your hand if you get scared."

"Deal." Who was I to turn down an opportunity to hold hands?

In my mind, Mackenzie was shaking her head. *That's really pathetic, Cassie.*

"I know," I muttered. "I know."

"What?"

"Nothing." I smiled up at him. "Lead the way."

The entrance to the Key West Cemetery was between two white pillars flanked on either side by a wrought iron fence. A blue marker near the gate said it was established in 1847, after a hurricane damaged the previous cemetery located near Higgs Beach. And that was all I had time to read before Ty tugged on my arm. "C'mon."

"If you're that eager to get back to Charisma," I said, twitching my arm out of his grasp, "you can just leave me here on my own. I'm perfectly safe. There was a cop right outside the entrance when I walked by earlier."

He glanced over his shoulder. "What are you talking about? There was no cop outside."

"Earlier. When I was on my way to Captain Crow's."

"That doesn't mean he's here now," Ty said. "They move around, you know. C'mon. Things to do, people to see. Dead people."

He let loose with a very unconvincing muah-ha-ha sort of evil laugh, and finished up with a grin, his eyes and teeth glinting in the darkness.

"Fine." I let him pull me along, down the path between the gravestones and crypts, gleaming palely in the dark.

At home, cemeteries were flat. The gravestones were sunk into the ground so the caretakers could simply drive the lawnmower right over them. I guess it made tending the grass easy.

This was a different kind of cemetery. It wasn't flat at all. Nor was it organized in neat rows. All the gravestones stood up—even if some of them leaned like drunken college students on spring break. But there were tall monuments, and the ground was littered with what looked like sarcophagi.

As we walked along, Ty pointed to things. "This is the memorial for the sailors who died when the USS Maine went down in Havana in 1898. That brick building over there belongs to the Mitchell family. That tall gray stone back there is a memorial to William Curry. He was Florida's first millionaire. And this—" He stopped in front of a stone, "is the final resting place of General Abraham Lincoln Sawyer."

I blinked at it. That's what it said, all right. *Abe L. Sawyer, 1862-1939.*

"Obviously not the same Abe Lincoln who was president

during the Civil War."

Ty shook his head. "Old Abe here was a little person."

"A..." I lowered my voice, conscious of the un-PC term I was about to use, "midget?"

He nodded. "A circus performer. His final wish was to be buried in a man-size tomb."

"You're kidding."

"Nope. It's the kind of thing you remember."

Yes, it was.

We moved on, over ground that felt so spongy I halfway expected it to give way and spill us both into someone's grave. Many of the tombs had big cracks in them, and I wouldn't have been surprised if a skeletal hand had reached out and grabbed for my ankle.

"Scared yet?" Ty wanted to know.

"Not scared. A little uneasy, maybe."

"Wanna hold my hand now?"

"Yes, please." I slipped my fingers into his. They were reassuringly warm and dry.

Ty pointed out the final resting place of the man who supervised the building of the Key West lighthouse, and the first missionary to Cuba. And then there was the guy whose gravestone said he'd been a good citizen for 65 years; not as major an accomplishment as you might think when he turned out to have lived to be 108.

"Good God," I said, "what an epitaph!"

Ty grinned. "Wait until you see this next one."

He kept walking. "Back there somewhere—" He waved vaguely with his free hand, "is the tomb of Sloppy Joe Russell. Have you noticed there's a place on Duval called Sloppy Joe's Bar?"

"Sure." It was a Key West fixture. I had seen pictures of it when I'd done research before we ever set foot on the plane last week.

"Sloppy Joe was a friend of Ernest Hemingway. They went deep-sea fishing together. Rumor has it that Sloppy Joe was the model for Freddy in *To Have and Have Not*, and after he died, parts of the original manuscript were found at the bar."

"Wow." I put Sloppy Joe's on my mental list of places to see tomorrow. "But that isn't what you're going to show me?"

He shook his head. "It's around here somewhere..."

We had wound up in front of a large, black archway with the words *B'nai Zion* carved on it. "The Jewish cemetery," Ty said. "What we're looking for is over here."

He tugged me in the other direction, and I found myself standing in front of a crypt with a tablet. "There," Ty said triumphantly.

I peered at it, and then peered closer. "Oh, my God. Does that really say '*I told you I was sick*'?"

"Yep." He grinned. "This woman—I think her name was Pearl—was the town hypochondriac. There's one around here somewhere that says, '*Devoted fan of Julio Iglesias*,' too. And one that says, '*If you're reading this, you desperately need a hobby*.' "

"Wow."

"And I've heard rumors that there used to be one that said, '*At least I know where he's sleeping tonight*,' but I've never been able to find it. But it's a cool place." He looked around with satisfaction.

It was. I might come back tomorrow, in the light, when I could see everything better.

"No ghosts, though," I pointed out.

Ty shook his head. "Sorry. There are plenty of ghosts in Key West, but I guess none of them are here tonight."

"I met a guy earlier who said he was Someone Jehosephat Windsor," I said. "I mean, he was the tour guide. He was pretending to be this Jehosephat Windsor. But he said Jehosephat haunts some place called the East Martello Fort. Some sort of museum?"

Ty nodded as we strolled hand in hand down the path between the monuments. "Now *that's* a creepy place. I was there once, and I wouldn't have minded a hand to hold. I think

I probably held my mother's."

I smiled. "What was so creepy about it?"

"Not old Jehosephat, or his hearse. As a matter of fact..." He stopped and looked around, and then pointed. "See that, over there? That's the Otto family plot. There are three Yorkshire terriers and a pet deer buried there, along with members of the Otto family."

"OK," I said.

"They had a kid named Robert Eugene Otto. And Robert Eugene had a doll, also named Robert. And Robert the Doll is in the East Martello Fort."

I tilted my head. "Why?"

"You ever see the movie *Chucky*?"

"I'm not really big on horror." Romantic comedy is more my speed. That and costume dramas. Although I know about the Chucky movies. Who doesn't?

"Chucky is based on Robert the Doll," Ty said. "Apparently he curses people who don't ask nicely enough if they can take his picture."

"You're kidding."

"No. There's a wall in the museum full of letters people have written, apologizing for being rude and asking Robert to remove the curse."

"Wow."

Ty nodded. "He moves around, too. Or so they say."

We walked a few paces in silence.

"You don't really believe that, do you?" I asked.

He glanced at me. "I believe in evil."

I guess I did too, if it came down to it. It was hard to be my father's daughter and feel differently. If you accept that there's good, you have to accept that there's evil. Can't have one without the other.

However, that wasn't the problem here.

"But that's different," I said. "That's people. People can be evil. And people can do evil." Like whoever had raped that poor girl this morning. "But objects aren't evil. They're just objects."

Knives and guns weren't evil. They could be used to do evil things, but by themselves there was nothing evil about them. And even something like a voodoo doll wasn't evil in and of itself. People who believed in that sort of thing stuck pins in the doll to harm the person the doll was supposed to represent, but the doll itself wasn't evil.

Ty shrugged. "Some people think Eugene Otto was so mean he turned the doll evil. He blamed everything that went wrong on the doll. And some people say the old Bahamian woman who made the doll cursed it."

"I don't believe in curses," I said.

Ty glanced at me, and then he grinned. "I don't either. But just the same, maybe you should be especially nice to Robert if you go on the ghost tour tomorrow. There's enough evil in Key West this week without inviting more."

There was, at that.

I promised I'd be extra careful, and extra nice to Robert the Doll if I saw him, and we left the cemetery and continued on our way toward the hotel.

CHAPTER *Five*

Ty stopped outside the hotel door as usual. "Here we are. Safe and sound."

Yes, indeed. I glanced over my shoulder into the lighted lobby, where people were walking around, and decided against inviting him up to my room. I knew what he'd say, after all.

"Thanks for the tour," I told him instead.

He smiled. "You're welcome."

"If you change your mind about going sightseeing tomorrow, you know where to find me."

He nodded.

"Although I won't hold my breath."

There was a pause. "It isn't that I don't wanna spend time with you, you know."

Could have fooled me, I thought. "Sure," I said.

He drove his hand into his hair and closed his fist. It looked like it hurt. "I like you, Cassie, OK? I'd like to spend time with you. I just... can't."

He actually sounded like he meant it.

So...

"Girlfriend?" I asked.

He looked torn. But eventually he nodded. "Yeah."

I nodded too, even as disappointment curled into my stomach and settled there. "That's OK."

Except it wasn't, of course. I didn't want him to have a girlfriend. The knowledge that he had a girlfriend made me sad. And the fact that he liked me, but couldn't do anything about it because he had a girlfriend, made me mad.

And what kind of girlfriend lets her boyfriend go to Key West on spring break on his own, anyway?

Not a very good one.

Or perhaps one who trusted her boyfriend to do the right thing, even when she wasn't around.

Anyway, I'm not the kind of girl who tries to steal another girl's boyfriend. So I simply told him, "Goodnight, Ty," and turned away.

And he told me "Goodnight, Cassie," and went off down the street.

And that was that. I went inside and up to bed. Alone.

I woke up early again the next morning, but I didn't walk on the beach. For one thing, I didn't want to risk finding another naked girl.

Not that it was likely I would, I suppose, although you can't be too careful.

But for another thing, I had breakfast plans with Mackenzie and Quinn.

When Mackenzie set up the rules for this trip, she had decreed that we were to see as little as possible of each other, so we could have the freedom to get properly laid. But she had built in this one meeting about halfway through the week, for us to dish and update each other on what we'd accomplished.

I was the first one to the dining room, not surprisingly. The others had found guys, and presumably guys who kept them busy at night. While the guy I'd found, walked me to my door at ten o'clock and left without so much as a kiss.

Because he had a girlfriend at home.

After Ty left last night, I'd lain awake for a while thinking about that.

I had fallen—might as well admit that—for a guy who was someone else's boyfriend.

A guy who was still choosing to spend time with me. He could leave me entirely alone. He probably should, especially since he'd admitted to 'liking' me. But he didn't. He sought me out instead. He was the one who'd picked me up in the bar that first night, and instead of letting me leave Captain Crow's alone yesterday, he'd come after me. He'd teased me, and held my hand, and showed me the cemetery, and told me he believed in evil.

That was some pretty personal stuff. In some ways, maybe even more personal than exchanging bodily fluids in bed. Or at least personal in a different way.

"That don't look like the face of someone who's just spent the night having wild monkey sex," Mackenzie's voice drawled, and I dragged myself back to reality as she scooted into the booth across from me, that damn sunhat still covering most of her face.

I grimaced. "You got that right."

"What happened?" She looked around for the waiter, probably to ask for some Southern iced tea. "The guy I saw the other night didn't look like he was the type to waste time."

"You wouldn't think so." Not to look at him. He'd certainly picked me up easily enough.

Mackenzie looked at me, arching her brows, and I added, reluctantly, "He has a girlfriend."

"No way!"

"Yes. Unfortunately."

"Damn, girl." She shook her head. "You sure can pick 'em."

"I didn't pick him," I muttered. "He picked me."

She tilted her head. The hat tilted too.

"Would you mind taking that damn thing off?" I added,

annoyed. "I like to see your face when I talk to you."

"Funny, that's what Austin said, too." She took the hat off and shook her hair out.

"Austin's the guy you were with at the pool yesterday? The guy from the bar the other night?"

She nodded. "Never mind about Austin. Why'd this guy pick you up if he already has a girlfriend?"

"I don't know," I said.

"Obviously not for sex. Not if you're not getting any."

I shook my head. "He says he likes me."

"Of course he does." She rolled her eyes. "You know what your problem is, Cassie? You're too damn nice. Guys all like you, and want to protect you, and things like that. But they don't wanna nail you to the wall and bang your brains out, do they?"

No, they didn't.

"If he has a girlfriend," I said, "I wouldn't want him to do that anyway."

We sat in silence a moment.

"It's only Tuesday," Mackenzie said. "You still have time to find someone else."

"I don't want anyone else," I muttered.

Mackenzie sighed. "No, of course you don't. This was supposed to be fun and games for spring break, Cassie. You weren't supposed to fall in love with anyone."

"I'm not in love with him," I said, and watched as Quinn turned into the dining room and stood for a second, looking around, before coming across the floor toward us.

"You sure about that?"

"Sure about what?" Quinn asked, stopping beside the table. I scooted aside to make room for her, since Mackenzie was sharing her half of the booth with the wagon-wheel sunhat.

She rolled her eyes. "Cassie's fallen in love."

"Oh. Good for her." Quinn slipped into the booth next to me.

"No, not good! He has a girlfriend."

"Bastard," Quinn said and turned to me. "What are you doing, messing around with a guy who belongs to someone else?"

"I'm not messing around with him! I can't even get him to kiss me, let alone do anything more." None of that wild monkey sex or nailing to the wall that Mackenzie mentioned. The kind of stuff she was probably getting.

The kind of stuff they were both probably getting.

"So not a problem, then." Quinn reached for the breakfast menu and opened it.

"Problem," Mackenzie said. "This was supposed to be a relaxing vacation. Nobody was supposed to fall in love."

"I'm not in love."

"I don't think you can decide that kind of thing ahead of time," Quinn said calmly. "Especially not for someone else." She closed the menu and put it down. "I think I'll have pancakes. With blueberries."

"Do they have cheese grits here?" Mackenzie grabbed for the menu. "How about biscuits and gravy? And sweet tea?"

"This is the south. I wouldn't be surprised." I reached for my own. "Just as long as there's orange juice, I'll be happy."

"It's Florida," Quinn said. "There'll be orange juice."

There was orange juice. And sweet tea. And everything else we'd asked for. Even Mackenzie's cheese grits that neither Quinn nor I would touch. And there was conversation. Lots and lots of conversation.

Mackenzie's new guy was Austin, and he was twenty-four. He worked as a bartender at Captain Crow's and picked up some extra money singing. Yesterday, after the pool, they'd gone upstairs to her room where he had relieved her of her virginity once and for all.

And Quinn had been spending time with Ivy League Dude aka James—although he wasn't Ivy League. He'd used to be, but apparently he'd been kicked out of Harvard or Princeton or Yale or one of those—I guess after partying too hard—and now he was at loose ends, going through his parents' money like water. He had rented a freaking villa for spring break, and invited all his friends down, and they were busy drinking all the Tequila in Key West and decimating the female population.

I sat back, ate my eggs, and let them talk. I didn't have much to contribute—we'd already discussed Ty, and the fact that he had a girlfriend—and besides, I was more interested in listening. And not just because I love my friends and want them to get what they want, but because I was puzzling over the girl on the beach and wondering whether either Austin or James was a likely candidate for roofies and rape.

Austin was local. He had tattoos and looked like a real bad boy—and that often includes some drug use, too. Sex, drugs, and rock'n roll. And he worked at Captain Crow's, where the girl—Elizabeth—had been seen the night before we'd found her. He'd had opportunity to doctor her drink, I assumed. And Mackenzie said he had walked her to her room, but although she'd tried her best, he'd refused to come in.

He could have gone back to the bar, or out on the town, and encountered Elizabeth. He could have taken her onto the beach and raped her.

I couldn't quite figure out why he would, when he could have had Mackenzie for the asking, but there's no explaining certain things. And as for motive... well, maybe he resented being local and having to work while all the rich kids came into town to party and throw money away. Maybe he resented being ordered around and expected to serve them. I could imagine how that might rub someone the wrong way, someone less privileged, who didn't go to college and who had to work for a living.

And James... I'd already wondered whether one or more of the group of Ivy League Dudes could be involved. Rich, privileged, used to getting whatever they wanted just by pointing to it. Recreational drug use is often part of that culture. And if he'd wanted Quinn and Quinn had said no—and it sounded like she had, at least at first—he might have decided to take out his frustrations on someone else.

But since I didn't want either of my friends to know what I was thinking—not until I had something more than crazy ideas to back me up—I didn't say anything, just listened and let them talk.

"James has a boat," Quinn said. "We went sailing all day yesterday."

Mackenzie whistled. "La-di-dah! What about today?"

"Sightseeing," Quinn said.

Good. Sounded like she'd be somewhere with lots of people around.

"What about you?" I asked Mackenzie.

"Snorkeling," Mackenzie said. "Austin knows all the best places. And swimming and sunning and sex." She winked.

"Be careful."

And I guess maybe I sounded envious or something, because they glanced at each other and then at me.

"What are you gonna be doing today, Cassie?" Mackenzie asked.

"Sightseeing, too." And on the way, I'd stop by Richardson's Motel, where Ty was staying, and talk to him about Austin and James, and about Mackenzie and Quinn. And if he thought the guys were something to be worried about, then I'd tell both my friends what I was thinking. And if that made them both hate me, then so be it. At least they'd be safe. "I'm going to see Hemingway House and Sloppy Joe's Bar and the Civil War fort and the haunted doll in the museum."

"Enjoy," Mackenzie said and plopped the outsized sunhat on her head. She wiggled her way to the end of the bench.

Meanwhile, Quinn scribbled her room number at the bottom of the receipt and scooted out of the booth, too. "Gotta run. James is waiting. Maybe we'll see you, Cassie."

"Have a good time," I said. "Don't do anything I wouldn't do."

They looked at each other. "No offense, Cass," Mackenzie drawled, "but that don't leave many options."

Perhaps not. I watched them as they walked out of the

dining room and parted ways in the lobby, and then I took the pen and wrote my own room number on the bottom of the check, and got out of there myself, too.

I stopped at the desk in the lobby to ask directions to Richardson's Motel. It turned out to be a mile or so away, on the opposite side of Captain Crow's. Ty had certainly gone above and beyond the call of duty in walking me home every night, when his own lodgings were in the other direction.

The woman behind the counter marked the location of Richardson's on a tourist map of the sights, and I set out, plotting my course.

Several of the places I wanted to see—including Hemingway House and Sloppy Joe's Bar—were on the way between where I was and Richardson's. But it was going on ten o'clock, so chances were Ty would be up by now. By the time I got over there, it would be ten thirty. If I waited much beyond that, he might go out and I'd miss him. So perhaps I should go straight to Richardson's instead of sightseeing along the way. The sights weren't going anywhere, after all, but Ty might.

I could see the lighthouse in the distance as I set out, and I made a decision to go see it later. It was located across the street from the Hemingway House, or so the map claimed, so it wouldn't be out of my way. I'm not afraid of heights, and the view would probably be spectacular.

And even though I wasn't consciously sightseeing, there was plenty to look at along the way. Lots of old houses and buildings: big Victorians, small bungalows and cottages, and the ever-present square beach houses with wraparound balconies on all floors. Many were white, but some were painted in the traditional beach colors, like pale blue and green, pink and yellow. There were palm trees everywhere, and huge bushes with enormous flowers.

And people. Lots and lots of people. Mostly naked people, or maybe that was the preacher's daughter in me. But I saw a lot more skin than I was comfortable with in broad daylight on a city street. I'd thought my own shorts and tank top were pretty skimpy, but compared to some of the people I saw, I was dressed for a blizzard.

Richardson's turned out to be a roadside motel of the old style. One story tall, painted gleaming white with turquoise doors all in a row, and a glazed pot with green leaves and red flowers outside each unit. I didn't see Ty sitting beside the pool, and I didn't know which room was his, so I headed for the office, located in a pointed A-style building in the middle of the complex.

The front desk was manned by a skinny guy with a scraggly beard and shifty eyes, wearing a Wizards of the Coast T-shirt. He was reading a comic book, one he tried to hide beneath the counter at the sight of me. Unfortunately, he fumbled getting it onto the shelf I assumed was there, and it fluttered to the floor, so he had to bend and pick it up. When he straightened, his pasty face was flushed, either with embarrassment or exertion.

"Hi," I said, smiling a friendly smile. "I'm looking for Ty McKenna."

Dude's brownish-green eyes flickered. "Room 102."

Excellent. "This way?" I pointed right, to the wing of rooms spreading in that direction.

He nodded, but didn't meet my eyes. I stopped halfway to the door, my spider senses tingling. "Is he there?"

He shook his head.

I walked back to the counter. "Where is he?"

"Police station," Wizard Dude muttered into the beard.

"Excuse me?"

"Cops came and got him couple hours ago."

My heart gave an uncomfortable lurch, or maybe that was my stomach clenching. Either way, some part of me wasn't happy to hear this. "Why?"

"Found another girl this morning," Wizard Dude said.

Oh, crap. "They did?"

WD nodded.

"Where? On the beach again?"

WD shook his head. "Cemetery."

Something cold skittered down my spine, as if one of the ghosts had run an ice-cold fingertip down my back. "The... the cemetery?"

We'd been at the cemetery last night.

But maybe that was a different cemetery.

"The old cemetery," Wizard Dude said. "On Passover Lane."

That was the cemetery we'd been in.

And that explained why the police had wanted to talk to Ty, I guess.

Although it didn't explain how they'd known we'd been there. I hadn't seen anyone I knew on the walk from Captain Crow's to the cemetery.

But of course the streets had been full of people. Just because I hadn't recognized anyone, didn't mean someone couldn't have recognized us. Or recognized Ty.

Maybe the cop from yesterday morning had still been around somewhere, and had seen us go in. Just because we hadn't seen him, it didn't mean he couldn't have seen us. And he would have recognized Ty from the beach yesterday morning.

Unless there was some other reason the police came to find him when another rape victim turned up.

Did they think he'd had something to do with it?

Was he a suspect?

He'd found the first victim. From the mystery reading I've done, I knew that that automatically meant he was a person of interest. The person who finds the body always is. And he had been in Captain Crow's at the time when Elizabeth had—or might have been—drugged.

He didn't have an alibi for the time of the rape, or at least none I had provided. He hadn't spent the night with me on Sunday.

He hadn't spent the night with me yesterday, either.

I shot Wizard Dude a glance from under my lashes, but he

was back to reading his comic again. He didn't seem all that interested in any of this, frankly.

I craned my neck and looked over the counter. The comic was the Japanese kind, and on the page he was reading, a scantily clad, big-eyed girl in a sailor suit was fighting off some many-tentacled octopus monster.

Or maybe not fighting it off, exactly.

Oops.

I blushed, and so did Wizard Guy. I guess maybe he wasn't too thrilled that I'd realized he was reading comic strip porn.

I didn't bother to apologize, just muttered a goodbye and made myself scarce as quickly as possible. But as I walked up the sidewalk away from the motel, I wondered whether someone's choice in reading material—and the fact that they apparently liked to watch big-breasted cartoon characters in skimpy dresses get sexually assaulted by octopi—might make them more or less inclined to sexually assault someone in real life.

CHAPTER Six

Instead of Captain Crow's Bar, I ended up at Captain Tony's Saloon that night.

Captain Tony's on Greene Street was what used to be Sloppy Joe's back in the days when Ernest Hemingway lived in Key West.

The building was constructed in 1852, as an ice house that doubled as the town morgue. After that, it became a telegraph station, a cigar factory, a bordello, and several speakeasies, before Joe Russell bought it in the 1920s, and started Sloppy Joe's Bar.

But in 1938, when the landlord raised the weekly rent by a dollar, Joe and his crew moved the entire operation around the corner to Duval Street overnight, and that's where Sloppy Joe's sits now. I'd stopped by in the afternoon, on my sightseeing jaunt through town, and that's when I'd learned all this.

In 1958, a local charter boat captain named Tony Tarracino opened Captain Tony's in the building where the original Sloppy Joe's used to be, and although Tony was dead and gone now, his namesake was still going strong.

By eight o'clock that night, I was sitting at the bar swilling Sprite, grinning at the very handsome, very flirtatious bartender. His name was Juan, and he had eyes like melting chocolate and lots of curly, black hair. Just what the doctor ordered. Nothing at all like Ty. If I played my cards right, I might even convince him to take me home... although I didn't intend to try. If there was one thing I'd learned from this situation, it was that I'm not the kind of girl who can go out and get laid for the purpose of getting laid—or the purpose of losing my virginity. When that happened, I wanted it to be with someone I cared about, and not just a guy I picked up in a bar because he was good-looking.

That's not to say I didn't enjoy talking to Juan. He seemed to enjoy talking to me too, about Key West history and about Captain Tony, who had been alive until Juan was in his late teens.

"Family?" I ventured.

He shook his head. "Just a Key West fixture. I was too young to tend bar then. And he didn't own the place anymore. But he'd come in and work the room." He smiled.

"That's cool. Did you always want to work here?"

He nodded. "This was the coolest place in the world to me, growing up. Jimmy Buffett got his start here, did you know?"

I didn't. I barely knew who Jimmy Buffett was. But I made encouraging noises, and Juan kept talking.

About halfway through the evening, one of the Key West patrol officers came in, and climbed up on the stool next to me. Juan provided him with a Coke and the greeting, "Enrique must be shitting bricks."

The cop, the same one I'd seen outside the cemetery the night before, on my way to Captain Crow's, nodded. "Fit to be tied."

Enrique... Fuentes?

Yes, I could well imagine Detective Fuentes being beside himself at this new development. Not just one girl one night, but two girls in two nights now. That was almost like a serial rapist, wasn't it?

It made me—and probably Ricky Fuentes—expect that another girl would be found naked somewhere in town tomorrow morning.

And it made me—and surely Ricky Fuentes—realize that right now, somewhere in Key West, some pervert was targeting another girl... and there was absolutely nothing either of us could do to stop it. There were too many vulnerable girls in Key West this week, and too many guys preying on them. No one could keep an eye on everyone.

"What about the FBI?" Juan asked. "How's that panning out?"

The cop snorted. "The FBI is useless."

And then he must have realized I was sitting here, because he shot a glance my way and clammed up.

"It won't hurt her to know what's going on," Juan told him. "At least she's one girl we don't have to worry about."

The cop nodded morosely. He looked like a vulture hunched over his glass, with a beaky nose and a small head on a skinny neck.

Juan added, "I still think Enrique shoulda gone out with the information instead of trying to take care of it quietly."

"It wasn't the detective's fault," the cop said, confirming my suspicion that Enrique was Detective Ricky Fuentes. "It was the brass. And the mayor. And the Chamber of Commerce. If we cancelled spring break, every business in Key West would suffer. Including this one."

Juan shrugged, conceding the point. "I still say people oughta know. If they wanna come here anyway, then it's on them."

The cop shrugged.

Neither of them said anything for a moment, so I ventured a question. "The girl this morning... does she remember anything?"

The cop shook his head. "Just that she was out on the town,

and then she woke up in the cemetery."

"I was there last night," I confessed. "Walking through on my way back to the hotel. Around ten."

"She probably wasn't there yet," Juan said. Smart guy; he'd figured out what I was thinking. "It probably happened later."

"So there wasn't anything I could have done."

They both shook their heads.

"I found the girl on the beach, you know. Yesterday morning." And Lord, didn't it feel like it was a lot longer ago than that? "What happened to her?"

"She flew home," the cop said. "This afternoon."

"And she never remembered anything, either?"

They both shook their heads.

"This is scary."

Juan smiled. "Just stick with us, Cassie. We'll make sure you're safe."

"Thank you." I sipped my Sprite. "I'm down here with two friends. They've both hooked up with guys they met here. I haven't seen either of them since this morning, and I'm a little worried."

They exchanged a glance. "Is either of your friends a blonde?" the cop asked, reaching out to touch the end of my hair with a fingertip. "Because so far, this guy seems to like blondes."

"Mackenzie is, usually. Darker than me, though. And she's dyed her hair brown for this week." They both looked at me, and I shook my head. "Don't ask. Anyway, Quinn isn't. Blond. She has dark hair and dark eyes."

"Who's the guy Mackenzie has hooked up with?" Juan asked with a glance at the cop.

"He's local. His name is Austin. He tends bar at Captain Crow's sometimes."

Juan smiled. "I know Austin. I don't think you need to worry about him."

"Oh. Good." That made me feel a little better, anyway. Something tight loosened inside me. "Quinn's guy is here for spring break. James something. Some privileged Ivy League dude with a villa and a sailboat."

They both shook their heads. "Haven't come across him," the cop said, and it was hard to tell whether the tone of his voice was disappointment or satisfaction.

"Look at it this way," Juan told me, "if your friends are with these guys, chances are they're safe. It's the girls who are out on the town partying who have to be careful."

Like me. Except I was forewarned and forearmed, so chances were nothing would happen to me. It was one of the girls who didn't know what was going on who was going to fall victim to this creep.

Yeah, I agreed with Juan. They should have gone out publicly with this information. At least that way, people would have been aware.

Juan's eyes fastened on something over my shoulder, and the corners of his mouth turned down. "*Madre de Dios, 'mana. Abuela* would roll over in her grave if she could see you."

I turned my head, and found myself face to face—or nose to chest—with Charisma, the drama student from Syracuse.

Who was busy sticking her tongue out at Juan.

"I'm sorry," I told him, "what did you call her?"

He looked at me. "Nothing bad. '*mana*. Short for *hermana*."

I nodded. That's what I'd thought. My Spanish was a bit rusty, but it was one of the first words I'd learned, ten or so years ago, in middle school.

La familia.

Padre, madre, hermano, hermana.

Father, mother, sister, brother. Or brother, sister, more accurately.

Abuela meant grandmother. The one who was spinning in her grave.

"You're siblings?" I said.

They both nodded, and now that I saw them together, the family resemblance was obvious. Same big eyes, same high cheekbones, same full lips.

And with that fact established, they went back to their conversation. "I'm just trying to fit in, *gordo*," Charisma said. "Enrique has drafted everyone he knows to hang out in bars this week."

Enrique again. Ricky Fuentes.

Who looked a lot like both Juan and Charisma—or whatever her name was—now that I thought about it.

"Is Detective Fuentes also your brother?"

"Enrique, then Alma, then Lupe, then Juan, then me," Charisma said.

"Carmen," Juan added.

Right. Carmen. Charisma. Close enough.

She was wearing another skimpy tank top tonight, along with a pair of cutoffs that barely hid her butt, and on her feet a pair of strappy sandals with ridiculously high heels. Somehow she managed to make the outfit look great, even if the shirt proclaimed, *Weapons of Mass Distraction* across her chest.

"I saw you yesterday," I said. "At Captain Crow's." With Ty.

She nodded. "I was there." And then she took a closer look at me and seemed to realize something. "Oh."

Yep. That was me. The one he left you for.

"Enrique asked me to keep my eyes open," Charisma—Carmen—said, with a shrug that set those weapons of mass distraction bouncing, "so I stuck close to Ty. I figured if anything was gonna happen, he'd be the one to watch."

Right. My mouth tasted sour, so I drank some more Sprite. Next to me, the cop finished his Coke and slid off the barstool. "I should get going. Back to work."

Juan nodded. "See you, Stan. Keep your eyes open out there."

Stan lifted a hand and ambled off toward the door, all skinny arms and legs with outsized feet and hands. Carmen said something to Juan, but it was low enough and fast enough—and Spanish enough—that I didn't catch it. I sucked Sprite through my straw, morosely.

"So you and Ty," Carmen said, "you're together?"

I shook my head. “Oh, no. No, we’re not. Just friends. He has a girlfriend in Washington.”

“Oh.” She looked at Juan, who looked back at her with a grimace. Carmen turned back to me. “I thought, when he left Captain Crow’s so fast yesterday...”

“We’re just friends. He walked me back to the hotel. And then he left without going inside.”

“Have you seen him today?”

“I went looking for him,” I admitted, “but he wasn’t there. The guy at the motel told me the police had come and picked him up.”

They both nodded. “Enrique isn’t the type to waste time,” Juan said.

Obviously not. “Do you know anything about the guy who works at Richardson’s Motel? Wizard Dude? He was reading Japanese cartoon porn.” With tentacles. Eww.

Carmen turned her lips down, and looked ridiculously like her brother for a second. “Ronnie Briscoe. Reading about it is about all he’s capable of. He’s a little weird, but generally harmless. I think.”

I nodded. I was really just scrambling frantically to come up with a suspect that wasn’t Ty.

Not that I thought Ty had it in him to drug and rape someone. Not when it came right down to it. But it seemed maybe the police did. And it was possible they knew something I didn’t.

Was it significant that I had been a blonde in a pink dress that first night he picked me up, and a blonde in a pink dress had been raped later on?

And was it significant that a girl had been raped and left in the cemetery the same night he’d taken me there?

Was it possible that there was something seriously wrong in his head, so that he could walk me back to my hotel, acting like the nicest guy in the world, and leave me on the doorstep even when I asked him to come upstairs, and he could go and viciously rape some other girl just for the crime of looking like me or being where I'd been?

It didn't seem likely—not the guy I knew, or thought I knew—but at the same time, it was hard to be sure. I didn't really know him, after all. A couple of hours over two days isn't enough to get to know someone, even if it is enough to imagine yourself in love with him.

A glass materialized on the bar in front of me. Stemmed, with pink liquid inside, and a little blue umbrella hanging over the side. "On the house," Juan told me with a wink. "You look like you could use something stronger than Sprite."

I eyed it suspiciously, and he chuckled. "Don't worry, *querida*. It's practically virgin. Just looks more festive than what you've been drinking."

"If you've made it this far," Carmen chimed in, "we don't want nothing to happen to you now."

No, we didn't. I took a sip from the glass, and when I couldn't taste the alcohol, decided it was probably OK.

One turned into two, but although I felt a tiny little buzz in my veins, it was no more than that first night at Captain Crow's when Ty picked me up. I sat and listened to Carmen—who wasn't a drama student at Syracuse, obviously—tell Key West ghost stories, egged on by her brother.

"Did you make it to the Audubon House today?" she asked me.

I shook my head. "The bird guy?"

She nodded. "He was here and in the Dry Tortugas in the 1830s, and drew a lot of birds. Captain Geiger, who was the original owner of the house, is said to walk. They say he's guarding his fortune."

"Where's his fortune?"

"Buried somewhere in the grounds," Carmen said. "And his daughter Hannah's portrait is haunted. They had to move it out of the public part of the museum because it made people sad."

A haunted portrait. I couldn't quite determine whether that was better or worse than a haunted doll.

"The Hard Rock Café used to be the Curry Mansion. Did Ty show you William Curry's gravestone when you were in the cemetery yesterday?"

"I think he might have mentioned it," I said, since the name sounded familiar. It wasn't one we'd stopped at, though.

"Curry was Florida's first millionaire. He built the house for his son Robert."

Obviously there were a lot of men—and dolls—named Robert in Key West history.

"But when William passed away and Robert inherited all the money, he couldn't handle the responsibility. He committed suicide in one of the bathrooms after losing the entire fortune."

Yowch. "So the Hard Rock Café is haunted?"

Carmen nodded. "And at Fort Zachary Taylor, down at the state park, you can see ghost soldiers lining up in formation and hear gunshots and whistles."

"Wow." That was one of the places I had planned to go today, that I hadn't made it to. After hearing that Ty was at the police station, I'd been a little distracted, to be honest, and hadn't gotten as much done as I had wanted. I figured I'd go back out tomorrow, to see some more.

"And has anyone told you the story of Count von Cosel and Elena?"

Juan rolled his eyes.

"No..." I said, watching him.

Carmen smiled. "You'll like this. A man named Karl Tanzler, who sometimes called himself Count Carl von Cosel, worked as an X-ray technician at the Marine Hospital in Key West in 1931. He fell in love with a girl named Elena Milagro de Hoyos, a Cuban immigrant. Karl was in his fifties, and Elena was twenty-two, and dying of tuberculosis. He tried to cure her with a concoction of gold leaf and water."

For tuberculosis? "That's crazy."

"Tell me about it," Juan muttered.

"When he proposed, Elena turned him down. But after she died, he talked her family into letting him build a mausoleum for her. And then he started visiting her every night, bringing her flowers and gifts."

"That's weird."

"It gets weirder," Juan said with a scowl at his sister. Carmen grinned.

"After two years, Karl took Elena's body out of the tomb and into an old airplane fuselage behind the hospital, where he began to 'restore her to life' with wire and plaster of Paris and glass eyes."

Eww!

"And when he learned that the military was planning to get rid of the old airplane, he moved her to his house on Flagler Avenue. And lived with her there until 1940."

Double eww! "Lived with her? You mean, her corpse?"

"Held together with wire and plaster of Paris," Carmen nodded. "And dressed in a wedding gown and veil."

"That's..." *Unbelievable. Disgusting. Grotesque.* I lowered my voice. "He didn't... sleep with her, did he?"

"I imagine he did," Carmen said calmly. "Apparently he inserted a paper tube for easy access."

Oh, gack. That went well beyond eww. I was practically gagging, and I swear all the blood drained out of my head.

"Eventually people caught on, of course, and he was arrested and charged with grave robbery and abusing a corpse. But because the statute of limitations had run out, he wasn't convicted."

"That's sick."

Juan nodded.

"After he got out, he charged people twenty-five cents to tour his house and see the lab where he'd worked on Elena."

I stared at Carmen.

"And the authorities decided that there was so much interest in the remains, that they put them on display to let people see them."

"Ghouls," Juan muttered.

"And after that, they put Elena in a metal box and buried

her in an undisclosed location, so Karl wouldn't dig her up again. He ended up blowing up the mausoleum he'd built, and then moving to Zephyrhills, where his ex-wife lived. He died in 1952, supposedly clutching a life-size replica of Elena. Some people say it was suicide, but he was in his seventies by then, so I'm not sure."

"That's..." I shook my head. I had no words.

"I know." Carmen grinned. "Isn't it great?"

Sure. Great.

"I think I should go home now," I said, sliding off the stool and onto the floor. It tilted, and I had to brace myself on Carmen's shoulder. "Sorry."

"You OK, Cassie?" Juan asked, his brows lowered. "Maybe you should go with her, Carmen."

"She'll be fine," Carmen said. "Just as soon as she gets outside."

Juan contemplated her, then nodded. "If you say so."

"Trust me."

He obviously did, because he nodded. "Come back and visit, Cassie."

I promised I would, and then I made my way across the floor toward the door while I wondered what that last exchange had been all about. I mean, of course I was fine. I could walk a fairly straight line, and I was certainly no worse off than a lot of other people. I was considerably more sober than most.

I hiked my purse more firmly over my shoulder, pushed the door open, and stepped through.

CHAPTER *Seven*

Waking up hurt. My head felt like the entire UC drum line was practicing inside, along with the cheerleaders, and my tongue stuck to the roof of my mouth like it was glued there.

But I drank the water.

My brain stuttered for a second.

What water?

I hadn't been drinking water. Or even Sprite. Juan had served me some sort of pink drink with a blue umbrella.

So much for his assertion that whatever it was, was practically virgin.

Except... I'd only had a tiny little buzz on when I left the bar, hadn't I? It wasn't like I couldn't remember everything that happened. Juan had been serving me drinks on the house, and Carmen had been talking about ghosts and then told me that awful story about Count Carl and Elena. I'd decided to go home—back to the hotel—before she could come up with something even more horrible, and Juan had suggested that maybe Carmen should go with me.

She'd said no; that I'd be fine as soon as I got outside.

And I had been fine. The cooler air had helped to clear my head. I'd set off down the street toward the hotel, and...

Everything after that was blank. If someone had given me water between there and here—and I did have a vague mental image of a voice telling me, "Here. Drink this. You need to rehydrate"—I didn't know who it was.

But maybe it was just a dream. Shades of Karl Tanzler making Elena drink his concoction of gold leaf in water to cure her tuberculosis.

That'd explain why my mouth felt like the Dust Bowl in August.

I slitted my eyes and peered out. The sunshine hit my eyeballs like a laser scalpel, and I squeezed them shut again with a moan. But I'd seen enough. I was in my own room in the hotel. The bedside table had the same glass lamp with an orange shade, and over in the corner was the same chair with pink and orange flowers.

Somehow I had made it here, even if I couldn't remember how.

And I guess I'd managed to get out of my shoes and jeans on arrival, although I was still dressed in underwear and my T-shirt.

A soft sound tickled the edge of my consciousness. The rustle of fabric. Or maybe a careful tread on the fluffy rug.

I forced my eyes open again. If I wasn't alone, I'd like to know about it.

A dark figure loomed over me. I squeaked and flopped over on my back, clutching my blanket to my chest for protection.

"Good," a voice said. "You're awake. Finally."

That voice...

"What are you doing here?"

Speaking of voices, mine was a croak. And using it made my head pound. I whimpered.

"Here." A glass of water and a couple of pills appeared on

the bedside table. The glass hit the hard surface with a click, and the pills rattled. The tiny sounds were magnified to roars in my pounding head. The voice continued, "Take this. You need to rehydrate. And the aspirin will help with the headache."

"That's what you said last time," I whispered. "And look what happened."

"What?" Ty said.

"I'm not sure I trust you."

He took a step back, and I got a better look at him. He looked tired, like he hadn't slept. Maybe he hadn't, if he'd been here all night.

I did a quick scan of my body, but best as I could tell, the only thing that hurt was my head.

His T-shirt was white today, with red letters above and below a red cross.

Not a religious cross; the square kind. A Red Cross kind of cross. At first my eyes refused to focus, but after a few seconds' concentration I could make out the words. *Virgin Search and Rescue Team.*

"Appropriate." I flopped a hand at it.

He glanced down, and then up at me. "Excuse me?"

"I'm still a virgin, right?"

Ty's eyes widened. "What?"

"Nothing." God, how stupid can you get?

He sat down on the edge of the bed next to me. The mattress gave a little, and the letters swam in front of my eyes. "If you were a virgin when I put you to bed, you're still a virgin."

Figures. "What are you doing here? Why'd you put me to bed?"

"Take the aspirin," Ty said, "and I'll tell you."

Fine. I reached for the glass and then hesitated with my hand halfway there.

He watched me. "You want me to dump it and fill it again?"

"No. I trust you." I did, even though I knew I shouldn't. Probably shouldn't. Didn't know enough about him to trust him.

But whatever else had happened last night, I was still intact this morning. He'd had his chance to do whatever he wanted to me, and he hadn't. So the water in the glass was probably just water.

I forced the pills down. The cold liquid slid into my stomach, leaving a chill through my chest on the way. I scooted up against the pillows and hugged one to my chest. "What happened?"

"I was hoping you'd tell me," Ty said.

I shook my head, and then wished I hadn't. "I have no idea. I don't remember anything after I left Captain Tony's. I don't even know where you came from."

He lowered his brows. "How much did you have to drink?"

"Not much. I started with Sprite. About halfway through the evening, Juan started feeding me these pink drinks with umbrellas. But he said they were mostly virgin."

"So d'you remember leaving Captain Tony's?"

"Sure." I nodded, very carefully. "Juan thought that maybe Carmen should go with me, but she said I'd be fine as soon as I got outside. And I was. I remember walking down the street, and then... nothing."

"You don't remember me? Or the cop?"

I shook my head. "What cop? Stan?"

"I guess that's his name. Tall, skinny guy with a big nose. He was at the beach that morning."

"Sure," I said. "I remember him. He sat in the bar for a while. Had a Coke."

"But you don't remember seeing him after you left?"

"No... Did I see him after I left?"

He sighed. "When I caught up to you, he was walking you home. You were stumbling and slurring your words like you were bombed out of your mind."

"I wasn't! You can ask Juan if you don't believe me." Unless Juan had lied about how potent the drinks were.

But I remembered leaving the bar. I'd been fine then. A tiny bit tipsy, but fine. It was what happened afterward that I couldn't remember.

"Stan said he'd seen you stumbling down the street and he thought he'd better take you home. But he didn't know where you were staying. He was going in the wrong direction when I saw you. So I took over and got you here myself."

He paused. I wondered whether I ought to thank him, but I wasn't quite ready for that yet. Especially since Stan would have gotten me here too, once he figured out where 'here' was.

"What were you doing there?" Coincidence, or...?

"Carmen called me," Ty said.

And that was another thing we had to talk about.

"You told me her name was Charisma. And that she was a drama student from Syracuse."

He ducked his head, and I swear his cheeks flushed. "Sorry about that."

"Why would you lie about something like that?" Whether her name was Charisma or Carmen, and whether she was a college student from Syracuse or a local here in Key West, it made absolutely no difference that I could see.

"I can't tell you that," Ty said.

I stared at him. It hurt my eyes to open them that wide, but I did it anyway. "What do you mean?"

"I mean I can't tell you why. Just that it seemed like a good idea at the time."

"Did you think I'd be jealous, or something?"

"No," Ty said, his lips curving. "Were you?"

"Of course not."

"Of course." But he was still grinning.

"You have a girlfriend in Washington," I reminded him. "It doesn't matter whether I was jealous."

The smile dropped off his face. "Right."

"Unless you were lying about that, too."

And it was embarrassing how much I wished he'd tell me he was.

He didn't. "Why would I lie about something like that?" he asked instead.

"I have no idea," I answered. "Why would you lie about Carmen's name?" Especially when there was a good chance I'd find out.

He sighed and shoved a hand through his hair. "I need you to trust me, Cassie. OK?"

"I do trust you," I said. "Why d'you think you're still here?"

I hadn't called the cops and had him dragged out yet, had I? And I totally could. He was in my room. Had maybe—probably—spent the night in my room.

And I wasn't even freaking out. Much.

"Then just..." He stopped and shook his head. "I was stupid, OK? You asked and I panicked, so I made up a story, because I couldn't tell you the truth."

I blinked. "Why not?"

"I can't tell you that."

Of course. "So why should I trust you? If you lied to me then, and you'll keep lying to me now?"

He leaned forward, those green eyes intense on my face. "I won't keep lying to you. I still can't tell you the truth—at least not right now—but I'll try not to lie again."

After a second he added, "Although maybe it's best if you don't ask too many questions."

Right.

I thought about it. It would have to be acceptable, since it was the best I was likely to get. "So Carmen called you. What did she say?"

"That you were at Captain Tony's sucking down Sex on the Beach, and I should come take you home."

I nodded. He hadn't had any problems answering that, anyway, and he sounded like he was telling the truth. Then again, he'd sounded like he was telling the truth when he told me about Charisma, too.

"But you weren't there when I left," I said.

He shook his head. "I got... delayed."

"By what?"

"That's another thing I can't tell you."

I tilted my head to look at him. The aspirin had kicked in and the drummers in my head had marched off across the field. I could still hear them, but faintly now. "I went looking for you yesterday. At Richardson's."

"You did?" He looked surprised, and not necessarily in a guilty way.

"I wanted to talk to you about something. But you weren't there."

I waited for him to volunteer where he'd been, but when he didn't, I added, "The guy at the front desk said the police had picked you up."

He nodded.

"Can you tell me about that?"

He shook his head. "Afraid not."

"Do they think you had something to do with the girls they're finding?"

"No." And from the way his lips twitched, it looked like he thought the question was funny.

"Do you?"

The smile slipped. "No. If I did, you wouldn't still be a virgin this morning."

Right. "It could just be that I'm not your type."

He didn't miss a beat. "Then those other girls wouldn't be my type either. They both looked like you, Cassie. Blond and sweet."

I wrinkled my nose. "Sweet?" Not sure whether to take that as a compliment or the opposite, but I suspected it was an insult.

"Virgins," Ty said.

"Tattooed across my forehead. Right. I forgot." I rolled my eyes. It only hurt a tiny bit. Yay for aspirin.

His lips twitched. "You don't have 'virgin' tattooed across your forehead. You just don't have 'do me' written across your chest."

"If I did, I'd probably get laid more."

"Probably. But—" He stopped.

I squinted at him. "But... what?"

"Nothing." His cheeks were flushed. "You're missing the point, Cassie. They were virgins. Both of them. Young, blond virgins."

Like me.

"So what happened last night?" I asked.

He ran a hand through his hair, frustration rolling off him in waves. "I don't know. Sometime between the time you left Captain Tony's and when I caught up with you, someone got something into you."

"A drug."

He nodded.

"So why wasn't I raped?"

"Dunno," Ty said. "Whoever did it lost control of you? The drug didn't work as fast as he'd expected? Or someone interrupted him before he could get you somewhere out of sight?"

Pick one. Any one.

I grabbed my head with both hands. "I wish I could remember. It's so frustrating not to remember! But after I left the bar, it's all blank."

"That's not unusual," Ty said. "None of the others remembered anything, either."

We sat in silence for a moment. "So where was I when you caught up with me? How far from Captain Tony's?"

"Couple blocks," Ty said. "Just a few minutes' walk if you didn't stop anywhere. Down past Sloppy Joe's a bit. Did you stop in there?"

"I could have. Although I was there in the afternoon. I don't see why I would have gone back at night. I remember wanting to go home. There was this story Carmen told me that totally freaked me out. About this local guy who dug up a corpse and lived with it in his house for years and years..."

He was nodding before I'd finished speaking. "I know the story."

"It's true, then?" Part of me had really hoped it wasn't, that

Carmen had been yanking my chain, making up ghost stories for fun.

"Afraid so," Ty said. "But if it helps, neither of them is rumored to haunt the place."

"Good to know. Anyway, I decided to leave. Juan asked whether Carmen should go with me, but she said no; I'd be fine once I got outside..."

"She'd texted me," Ty said. "She knew I was on my way."

"I remember walking out, and turning right, but after that, there's nothing."

"So you don't know where you were when Stan the cop found you, or how you'd gotten there."

It wasn't a question. I shook my head anyway. "I have this vague memory of someone giving me a water bottle and telling me to drink, that I needed to rehydrate. Was it you?"

He shook his head. "By the time I caught up, Stan was practically dragging you down the street. Getting you to drink anything was the last thing on my mind. I just carried you here and put you to bed."

"Thank you."

He shrugged. "You're gonna have to go to the hospital, you know."

I opened my mouth to protest, and he talked over me. "I know you don't think you were assaulted, but they have to check. And they have to draw blood and try to figure out what it was you were given. And you have to do it right now."

There went my day of sightseeing. "What time is it, anyway?" I asked.

"Twelve-thirty," Ty said.

"In the afternoon?"

He nodded. "This stuff makes you sleepy. But if you wait much longer, there won't be any sign of it in your bloodstream."

I squinted at him. "You know a lot about this."

"Let's just say I study pharmacology."

"Does Georgetown have a program for pharmacology?"

"Probably," Ty said. "They have a program for everything

else."

I squinted at him. "I guess this is one of those things you can't tell me."

"Afraid so." He got up from the edge of the bed and tossed my jeans at me. "C'mon. Get ready."

"Can't I at least have clean clothes?"

"Easier to wear those," Ty said, "since they were what you were wearing last night. The police will want a look. Pack a change, though. For after."

I didn't ask him 'after what.' I had a feeling I knew.

"I suppose a shower is out."

"And washing. And brushing your teeth. And peeing. The hospital lab will want a urine sample. But you can do it all later."

He headed for the door. "I'll give you some privacy to get ready. Meet me in the lobby in five minutes. I'll arrange a ride."

"Don't leave on my account," I told his back. "You already saw my underwear last night, didn't you?"

He shot me a grin over his shoulder. "I did. Nice color." He winked.

I was still blushing when the door closed behind him.

CHAPTER *Eight*

The ride he arranged turned out to be a cop car with an impassive young officer behind the wheel. It wasn't Stan. It wasn't anyone I'd seen so far, or if I had, I hadn't noticed him. He didn't say a word on the drive through town, just gazed out the windshield while he maneuvered the car through the crowded streets.

It wasn't a long drive. We ended up at a women's clinic not too far from Richardson's Motel. The cop let us out without a word, and when I thanked him for the ride, he simply touched the brim of his hat and nodded.

"Are you staying?" I asked Ty when the car had driven away.

He shook his head. "Something I gotta do."

So he was just going to leave me here?

He must have seen the thought on my face, because he smiled. "Detective Fuentes is on his way. He'll wanna talk to you."

"But I don't remember anything!" I protested.

"Just tell him what you told me. You'll be fine." He gave my shoulder a squeeze.

I wanted him to come inside with me. I really did. I was a bit nervous about the whole thing, to be honest. Not so much about being interrogated by Enrique Fuentes—although that was a bit scary too—but about the whole examination thing.

Not that they'd let Ty be there for that.

Not that I'd want him there while they were poking and prodding my privates.

If anything was less likely to make a guy want to sleep with a girl afterward, I imagine it would be watching her go through a pelvic exam, complete with rape kit.

But a little bit of support going through the door would be nice, even if he had to leave immediately after that.

"You'll be fine." He took my hand. "But if you want, I can stay with you until they take you inside."

Thank you! "That'd be nice," I said demurely and walked up the stairs.

In the end, it turned out to be only a minute and a half. We walked into a small waiting room with blue chairs and copies of *Cosmo*, and approached the glass enclosure on the opposite wall. A young woman in pink scrubs looked up from the computer. "Can I...?" She stopped at the sight of Ty. "Oh."

Struck dumb, I suppose. I smiled, since I was holding his hand and she wasn't. "My name is Cassandra Wilder. I'm supposed to have some sort of examination."

She nodded, without taking her eyes off Ty. "Have a seat. Someone will be with you momentarily."

"Don't you want my insurance card, or something?"

That got me a quick glance, anyway. "Not yet."

Fine. I took a seat. Ty sat next to me and kept holding my hand. "You'll be fine," he told me again, his thumb tracing patterns on my palm. It felt so good my insides melted a little. "Tell Fuentes exactly what you told me. I've already told him everything I know. And he's talked to Juan and Carmen and

Stan. He just needs to hear what you know to put together the pieces."

"I'm not worried about that. I'm just not looking forward to the examination."

"You've been to the gynecologist before, haven't you?" He was perfectly comfortable talking about it, it seemed. Most guys my age—his age—probably wouldn't be.

Although actually, he seemed a little older today, with his face so drawn and tired. And more serious, too. Not at all like the guys I went to school with.

"Are you sure you're only twenty-two?" fell out of my mouth.

He blinked and opened his own. But before he could get any words out, the door opened. "Cassie? Dr. Johnson will see you now."

I got to my feet, but Ty kept hold of my hand. "Have dinner with me?" he said.

I opened my mouth and closed it again. And nodded.

"I'll be in the lobby of your hotel at seven. Stay there until then. Don't go anywhere without me."

I nodded. And then I let go of his hand and walked to the door where the receptionist was waiting.

The examination turned out to be no big deal. Dr. Johnson—a young, black woman with braids and a singsong Caribbean accent—came into the examining room and sat down to talk to me. "Hi, Cassie."

"Hi," I managed, still a little nervous.

"I want to talk to you about what we're going to do, OK?" Her voice was sweet and calm. Calming. Like I was about to have a meltdown any moment.

I nodded.

"The police think you were drugged yesterday, so we'll draw blood and take a urine sample that we will test for drug residue."

I nodded. Ty had already warned me about that.

"And I will have to do a pelvic exam and rape kit."

"I wasn't raped," I said.

She sat back on the chair. "I'm sure you would like to believe that..."

"No. I mean, yes. Of course I'd like to believe that." I'd like to believe that the other two girls hadn't been raped either, but that simply wasn't true. "But I wasn't raped. I know I wasn't."

Her voice became even kinder. "I know this is hard, Cassie. But..."

"No," I said. "It isn't. You can do your pelvic exam, but you won't need the rape kit."

"Cassie..."

"Look," I said, annoyed by the constant repetition of my name, especially in that oh-so-kind voice. "I'm a virgin, Dr. Johnson. Or at least I was last night. I'm pretty sure I still am. If I wasn't, I think there'd probably be some blood and some pain. So why don't we get this show on the road, and you can see for yourself?"

There was a moment of silence, and then she grinned. "Good for you, girl. All right, then. I'll check and make sure you're still a virgin, and if you are, then obviously we won't need to do the rape kit."

"Thank you."

"But you still have to pee in the cup and have your blood drawn."

I nodded.

"Why don't you go do that now, since I'll be poking at you."

Good idea. I took the cup and went to the bathroom. When I came back, there was a hospital gown ready for me on the examining table, and five minutes later, I had confirmation that my virtue was intact. Whatever else had happened last night, that hadn't.

I won't deny that it was a relief. I'd gone on this vacation thinking it might be a good opportunity to lose that pesky virginity once and for all, in a place where people didn't know me and hadn't already prejudged me. But I didn't want it to happen like this. When it happened, I didn't want to be drugged out of my mind, or so drunk I didn't know who I was with or what was going on. I wanted it to mean something, with someone I liked. Not some creep who decided I was his for the taking, just because he wanted me.

I wanted it to be Ty, to be honest, although he couldn't have made it any more clear that it wouldn't be. No matter how much he 'liked' me.

But while that made me sad, I still didn't want to go out and get laid by someone else, just so I could tell Mackenzie and Quinn I had been, when we were on the plane home on Saturday. I'd go to dinner with Ty instead, and enjoy his company, and if that was all I got this week, that and my continued virginity, then that was fine with me.

"You can get dressed again—" Dr. Johnson began, just as a shrill scream sounded outside.

We both jumped, and I clutched the hospital gown to my chest. "What on...!"

"Excuse me." She was out the door before I could finish the sentence. I scrambled into my clean clothes and put the dirty ones in the bag for Detective Fuentes to take to the forensic lab when he arrived. Even though I hadn't been raped, there might be some kind of evidence on what I'd been wearing. Something to point them toward who was doing this.

When I was dressed, I opened the door and ran out into the hallway.

The commotion was coming from a room down the hall. The screams had turned into hysterical sobs by now, and things had calmed down a little. I got to the door just in time to see a girl in a hospital bed, her face battered, slump back against the pillows as Dr. Johnson pulled a syringe out of her arm.

Next to me stood another girl, also blond, her eyes huge. When she noticed me there, she turned to look at me. Up and down. "You too?" she said.

"Um..." Another blonde. My height. My age. Sweet, as Ty would say, but for the haunted look in her eyes. "Yeah," I said.

She nodded. "I'm Jeanine."

"Cassie Wilder."

She looked back into the room, where the girl in the bed was breathing more calmly now, even as tears ran silently down her cheeks. Jeanine lowered her voice. "I heard they found her this morning."

Oh, God. I could feel the color leach out of my face. "This morning?"

Jeanine nodded, but before she could say anything, a shadow loomed up behind us.

Or not exactly loomed, although he did the best he could. "You two," Detective Ricky Fuentes said, "out." He pointed down the hallway. "Wait for me in the lobby."

It didn't occur to me to protest. I scrambled, with Jeanine right behind.

We sat in silence. I didn't feel like talking, not with what I'd just found out. Another girl had been raped last night, and beaten up, too, it seemed. And it should have been me. And although I was glad it wasn't, it seemed horribly selfish to be happy that another girl was in pain right now because I wasn't.

Had he—whoever he was—been angry that I'd gotten away from him, and he had taken it out on her?

Ricky Fuentes came back out the door after a few minutes, his face a half dozen degrees grimmer than it had been on Monday morning. "C'mon," he told us without slowing down, "we can talk in the car."

I got to my feet, and so did Jeanine.

"I wanted to talk to you together," Fuentes said when we were in the car and driving down the street back into the thick of the Old Town, "to see whether you might remember more together than separately. There's only the two of you who might be able to help me. The girl who was..." he hesitated, looking for the right word, "attacked on Sunday night has already left Key West. And you saw what happened in there."

We nodded. Obviously the girl who had been attacked—I assumed Fuentes wanted to avoid the words 'assaulted' and 'raped'—last night wasn't in a frame of mind to talk about it.

"Is she OK?"

Duh. Of course she wasn't OK. "I didn't mean..." I added, feeling stupid.

Fuentes shook his head. "I know what you meant. Physically, she'll recover. Emotionally, she's worn thin right now. It'll be a while before I can talk to her."

So he wanted to see what little tidbit of information he could squeeze out of us in the meantime.

"I don't know much," I said apologetically. "I don't remember anything between the time I left the bar and when I woke up."

Jeanine nodded.

"Nothing at all?" His eyes met mine in the rearview mirror.

"Um... I think maybe someone asked me to take a drink from a bottle of water. Ty said it wasn't him. But it could have been my imagination. Your... Carmen had been telling me about Count Carl and Elena, and I may have been dreaming."

He nodded. "Jeanine? Do you remember a bottle of water?"

Jeanine shook her head. "I was drinking shots of tequila. At Captain Crow's."

"With the Ivy League Dudes?" I said.

They both looked at me. "What?"

I blushed. "Just a bunch of guys who sit there all night doing shots of tequila. Rich guys. Or look like they are. My friend Quinn has been hanging out with one of them." Or vice versa.

"Names?" Fuentes said.

"I only know his. James Somebody Hunt. The second or third or something."

"Is your friend Quinn a blonde?"

I shook my head. "I'm not saying these guys had anything to do with anything. Just that they've been at Captain Crow's drinking tequila every time I've been there."

"That's reason enough to talk to them," Fuentes said, and

went back to Jeanine. "So you were doing shots of tequila. Then what?"

"Then nothing. I don't remember what happened after that. Until I woke up the next day in the cemetery."

Ugh. I tried to imagine the horror of waking up on the spongy ground, naked and in pain, surrounded by all those gravestones, and knowing that something had happened but unable to remember what.

"I'm sorry," I told her, and reached for her hand. She looked a little surprised for a second, but then she squeezed back.

"Thanks." She kept holding on to me as we navigated the streets.

Fuentes dropped her off at the entrance to her hotel. "You going home this afternoon?"

Jeanine nodded. "My mom's flying down to pick me up. She'll be here soon. I'm going to go upstairs and pack my things, and then wait in the lobby."

"D'you have someone who can wait with you?"

I'd barely had time to ask the question before the doors opened and three girls came rushing out, hair flying. They surrounded Jeanine and whisked her off inside.

"Guess she does," Fuentes said. I nodded.

He put the car back in gear. "You were very lucky, you know."

Tell me about it. "I'm aware of that, Detective."

"You really can't remember anything at all from last night?"

"Not aside from what I've told you. I spent the night at Captain Tony's with your... with Juan and Carmen. Stan was there for a bit too. Carmen texted Ty and told him I was there, and to come walk me home, but I left before he got there. He said he'd been delayed..."

I trailed off, thinking Fuentes might volunteer something, but he didn't.

"And that's the last thing I remember. I was drinking Sprite, and then I was drinking almost-virgin Sex on the Beach. I was a little bit tipsy when I left, but not so much that I would have been stupid. I don't drink much at all, usually."

He nodded. "That's what Juan said. You didn't stop anywhere on your way home?"

"Not that I can remember. But I don't remember anything after I walked out the door. Except for that bottle of water that may or may not have been imaginary."

"Can you tell me anything about the voice?"

I blinked at him in the rearview mirror. "The one who told me to drink the imaginary water? Why?"

"Because if you didn't ingest the drugs in the bar," Fuentes said, "and Juan, Carmen, and Stan all say you couldn't have; you had Carmen on one side of you, and Stan on the other, and Juan behind the bar—then the drugs must have been given to you later."

"Sorry," I said. "It was just a voice."

"Male?"

"I assume." Although to be honest, I couldn't even swear to that. It was seriously just a vague memory of a voice; a memory I might have imagined.

"Any kind of accent?"

"I don't think so."

"Had you heard it before?"

I blinked. "Maybe."

He perked right up at that. "Really?"

"Sure. If it was a real voice and I didn't imagine it, it had to have been someone I trusted, at least enough to take a water bottle from. I mean, I'm not stupid. I wouldn't have accepted a drink from a stranger. Even a bottle of water."

Fuentes nodded. "Makes sense. So whose voice would you recognize?"

"Not a lot of people in Key West. Quinn and Mackenzie. You, Juan, Stan, Ty, Barry—the bartender at Captain Crow's—Carmen, the bartender at Sloppy Joe's, the two guys who run the haunted trolley tours, the tour guide at the Hemingway House, the desk clerk at Richardson's Motel, the staff at my own hotel, a couple of the other guests who have talked to me, or to each other..."

"A lot of people."

Maybe. "But I wouldn't accept a water bottle from most of them. Not if I were myself."

"Who would you accept a water bottle from? If you were yourself?"

"You," I said. "Ty. Juan." Had to include him, since he was Ricky Fuentes's brother. And besides, I'd been accepting drinks from him all night yesterday. "Stan." Had to include him too, since he was Fuentes's colleague. "If I was sitting at the bar at Captain Crow's, Barry and Austin. If I was in my own hotel, the staff. But on the street? Not a lot of people."

"Did you go to Captain Crow's last night?"

I shook my head, and then amended the negative. "Not that I remember. Ty was there, and I didn't want to see him."

His eyes sharpened. "Why didn't you want to see A... Ty?"

A...?

"Personal reasons," I said.

He looked at me in the mirror, but when I didn't volunteer any more information, he didn't push.

A minute later we pulled up outside of my hotel, and I reached for the door handle. "Thanks for the ride."

"That your clothes from yesterday?" Fuentes asked, nodding to the bag in my hand.

"Yes."

"Leave it in the car. I'll get it to the lab."

I left it on the seat. "Can you tell me anything about the girl in the hospital?"

He looked at me in the mirror, and I added, "Jeanine said she was found this morning. Did he grab her after he lost me last night?"

Fuentes hesitated. "So it seems."

Oh, God.

"Stay safe," Fuentes said. "It looks like you're on this guy's radar. Don't give him another opportunity."

"I'm having dinner with Ty tonight."

Fuentes nodded. "Stay in the hotel until he picks you up. Don't go anywhere on your own."

I promised I wouldn't. "Detective..."

He nodded.

"Why do you think he beat her? He didn't hurt any of the others, did he?"

"Not beyond the sexual assault," Fuentes said. "They didn't fight back. Maybe she did. Maybe he didn't have enough of the drug left to give her a full dose, and so she realized what was happening and fought him."

Gah. Bad enough to get raped while you're unconscious or mostly unaware, but to be awake and aware and unable to stop it...

"Or maybe he was angry," Fuentes added. "If he'd chosen you, and then he lost you... he could have taken it out on her."

"You don't know?"

He shook his head. "You saw her. She's not in a position to tell me. I'm going back there after I drop your clothes off at the lab. Maybe by then I'll learn something."

I nodded. *Time to go*. He had places to go and people to see. "Thanks again."

"You have my card? Let me know if you remember anything else, or think of something you haven't told me."

I said I would, and then I got out of the car and watched him drive away before I went inside and up to my room to while away the rest of the afternoon with a book. Maybe I'd see if Mackenzie or Quinn were around. A little girl-time sounded like just the ticket right now.

CHAPTER *Nine*

Mackenzie was around, and I ended up in her room for part of the afternoon, talking about boys and clothes. Everything nice and normal, as if there wasn't a girl who looked like me lying in a hospital bed on the other side of town.

Unfortunately, things were not going all that well for Mackenzie and Mr. Tat. Things had started out great, but then they'd had a falling out, Mackenzie said, over some girl named Rachel. Someone Austin had feelings for, or still had feelings for, or maybe used to have feelings for—if he'd ever had feelings for her.

It was confusing. I'm not sure Mackenzie understood it, either. But she was upset. Didn't want to admit it, and kept telling me—and I'm sure herself, too—that it was for the best, that this way she could quit while she was ahead, before she fell for him... when it was painfully obvious she'd already fallen, and hard.

This vacation wasn't working out according to plan for any

of us.

She perked up when I asked for help with an outfit for tonight, though. Although when I accidentally let it slip about having gotten myself drugged last night, I had to talk her out of calling Quinn and bundling us all onto a plane for home tonight. Quinn was out somewhere with Ivy League Dude, actually having fun, and she needed that, after the year she'd had. I wasn't going to be the one to deprive her.

"I'm fine," I told Mackenzie, not for the first time. "I swear. Don't bug her."

She put the phone down. "All right. I won't call her. But I need details, please. Every. Single. One."

No problem. She was a blonde, too, the rest of the time. And she was America's Sweetheart, so someone might know that and make an exception for her. It certainly wouldn't hurt her to know what was going on, so she could look out for herself. Especially now that Austin wasn't around to do it.

Ty was in the lobby when I came downstairs at seven, and the look on his face when he saw me was pretty damn gratifying.

Granted, the last time he'd seen me, I'd just woken up from sleeping for twelve plus hours, with bed hair, a drug-induced hangover, and bad breath, so anything would have been an improvement. But I hadn't had much to do upstairs while I waited for seven o'clock to roll around, so I'd taken a little extra time with my hair and makeup.

And then, of course, there was Mackenzie's dress and shoes. She wears cowboy boots a lot of the time, but she cleans up well when she wants to, and this was a pair of strappy silver sandals that she'd probably worn to some award show or other sometime. The dress, meanwhile, was little and black and elegant, which makes Mackenzie look sexy as hell. I couldn't quite pull that off—sweet, remember?—but at least I was pretty sure I didn't look like a virgin.

Ty's eyes widened when he saw me. "Wow. You look...

different."

I tried to bat my eyelashes at him, but they stuck together. Stupid mascara.

"Is that good or bad?" I asked instead.

He smiled. "It isn't either. You look great, but you always look great."

"I didn't look great this morning." Or afternoon. Whenever I'd woken up.

"You looked fine this morning. Although you look better now." He offered his arm and I took it. He was wearing a button-down tonight, instead of the usual T-shirt, and I could feel the warmth of his skin through the thin fabric.

He walked me—not toward the doors, but toward the back of the lobby. "I hope you don't mind, but I made reservations at a restaurant in the hotel. I'm afraid to let you go outside."

He looked a little embarrassed to admit it.

"That's fine," I said, "although I'm not worried."

"I am. You seem to have attracted the attention of this guy. And since it's my job to keep you safe..."

I glanced at him. "What do you mean, it's your job?"

"We have to talk."

Ah.

We passed through the door into one of the several restaurants Mackenzie's five-star hotel could boast. The hostess dimpled at Ty.

"Reservation for McKenna," he told her. "Somewhere out of the way?"

She nodded. "Follow me, please."

The way she filled out her own LBD made me green with envy, and she didn't seem to have a problem walking on the heels, either. I was already wishing for my flip-flops. They may not be as pretty as the silver sandals, but they're a lot easier to get around in.

We ended up at a table for two in a dark corner, behind some sort of potted fern. Ty held my chair and then seated himself, with his back to the wall. I'm not sure how much of the room he could see, what with the fern and all, but he kept an eye out.

"Job?" I said again when we were seated.

He sighed. "Let's get the orders out of the way, OK? Then I'll tell you everything."

"Everything?" Even the stuff he'd told me he couldn't tell me, when I'd asked him why he was lying to me?

He nodded. "Yeah. Everything."

OK. I could wait a few minutes for that.

So we ordered drinks, and then we ordered food, and then the waiter deposited a plate of bread and a dish of some sort of olive oil on the table, and withdrew.

"Talk," I told Ty.

He nodded, but he didn't actually say anything until he'd broken off a piece of the bread and had dragged it through the olive oil and put it in his mouth and chewed... When he'd swallowed, he said, "I owe you an apology."

"OK." I was busy crumbling my own piece of bread. My stomach was churning, so it wasn't like I could eat it, but I needed something to do with my hands. "What for?"

"I've been lying to you since the first time we met."

"I know that," I said, looking at my pile of crumbs.

He shook his head. "You have no idea. I've been lying about everything."

"Everything?" Even that seemingly sincere, 'I like you too'?

Maybe he could read my mind, because his lips twitched. "Almost everything."

There was still hope, then. "OK..." I said.

"My name isn't Tyler Jackson McKenna. It's Ty Connor."

"But..." I'd seen his driver's license.

Granted, it isn't that hard to get a fake ID, but why bother? He couldn't possibly be younger than twenty-one.

Could he?

"And I'm not twenty-two."

Uh-oh.

"I'm twenty-five."

"Twenty-five?" It was better than nineteen, but four years older than me...?

"I'd show you my real ID, but I don't have it on me."

"I'll take your word for it," I said, which was probably stupid, when he'd been lying all along.

The way he smiled told me he knew it, too. "I don't go to Georgetown," he said. "I never did."

I had already sort of figured that out, or at least I had suspected it. From the moment when he'd told me that Georgetown *probably* had a pharmacology program. If he went there, he'd know. Right?

"I went to the University of Florida. Psych major. And when I was twenty-three, I applied to the FBI."

My mouth opened, but nothing came out.

He waited while the pieces realigned themselves in my head. It was uncomfortable, but things started to make sense, finally. "So..." I said when I thought I had caught up, "you're here because of the girls? The... rapes."

He nodded. But before he could go on, the waiter came back with our salad plates.

"There was a problem during spring break last year," he told me when the waiter had deposited the plates and left again. "Not as organized as this, but a couple of girls were drugged and sexually assaulted. The Key West cops never figured out who did it. But just in case the same thing happened this year, they wanted someone on-scene. So they called the FBI."

"And the FBI sent you."

He nodded. "I look younger than I am, so they've been sending me on a lot of undercover assignments in high schools and colleges and gangs and places like that."

"Isn't it dangerous?" Man, if I'd felt like he was out of reach before, he was as far away as the moon right now. Twenty-five and an FBI agent. He probably had a gun and a badge and everything.

He went undercover in gangs, for God's sake.

He shrugged. "Sometimes. But someone's gotta do it."

Sure, but... did it have to be him?

Then again, if it hadn't been him, I wouldn't have met him. And if he hadn't been doing it yesterday, it might be me in the hospital today, screaming, with bruises all over my face and my virginity stolen by someone I probably wouldn't have given it to willingly.

"So... does Detective Fuentes know who you are? And Carmen?"

He nodded. "Carmen's sort of my liaison with the police. She passes on anything I need to know from Fuentes. Nobody thinks anything of it if I'm talking to her."

I could totally see why. Plenty of reasons why any normal guy would spend time talking to Carmen.

"And Fuentes is the one who insisted on calling in the FBI. He didn't want a repeat of last year. He's beyond pissed that we can't get a handle on this guy."

I didn't blame him. "Do you seriously have no idea who it is? If it was going on last year too, it has to be someone who was here then as well, right?"

"If it's the same guy. Or guys. Like I said, it wasn't as organized then. And it isn't like this kind of thing is rare. Unfortunately." He chased a cherry tomato around his salad plate before spearing it with his fork and looking at it instead of at me. "Fuentes wants to think it's a visitor. Someone who was here for spring break last year, and who's back now."

"That makes sense." And it reminded me that I hadn't told him my theory about the Ivy League Dudes.

When I was finished, he nodded. "That's a possibility. Are you sure you aren't a psych major yourself?"

I shook my head. "English Lit. But I've read a lot of thrillers. And Quinn's studying to be a counselor. She talks about cause and effect and trauma and stuff like that."

He tilted his head. "So is she trying to save this guy? James?"

"I have no idea." Although it wasn't impossible. She does seem to gravitate to the walking wounded. The guys who need her. "But I know he's been here before. The family has a house, or he rents a house, or something."

"Last year, one girl was a brunette and the other a blonde. Just two. This year, they've all been blondes. And the way they've been left in public places almost makes it feel..."

He hesitated.

"Like he's thumbing his nose at you?" I suggested.

He nodded. "I was gonna say it feels personal, but yeah. Something like that. Or like he doesn't care that we know what he's doing. He's not trying to hide it. Last year, both girls woke up in their own rooms and went to the police when they realized what had happened. This year, he's almost putting them on display."

"Like he wants you to catch him."

"Or like he wants to play," Ty said and ate his tomato.

I picked at my own salad. This conversation had robbed me of what little appetite I'd had. "There could have been more girls last year. I'm sure you've thought of that. Girls who didn't realize what had happened, or didn't want to go to the police, or didn't want to admit that they'd been drugged and raped. And if they didn't report it, or think about it, it was like it hadn't happened."

He nodded grimly.

"This year, there's been a girl every morning so far, right?"

"Since Monday. There wasn't one on Sunday. Or Saturday night, I should say. Not sure what that means. If it means anything at all."

"If he's from out of town, it could mean he didn't get here until Sunday."

Ty nodded. "It could mean that."

We sat in silence for a moment.

"Why do you think there are only blondes this year?"

"Could be a different guy," Ty said. "Or could be he decided he liked blondes better. Maybe he enjoyed raping the blonde more last year."

He pushed his salad plate away. I did the same with mine.

This whole conversation was nauseating.

The waiter came and whisked the plates away as soon as he saw we were done. "The food will be right out," he told us before walking off.

I looked at Ty. "What do you think?"

"About the food?"

"About the guy. You keep saying 'could be this' and 'could be that,' and 'Fuentes wants to believe the guy's a visitor.' But what do you think?"

He hesitated. Looked at me, and chewed on his bottom lip. Hesitated some more. I waited.

"I think he's local," he said eventually. "I think he's someone who lives here, but who takes advantage of the fact that all of Key West is crazy this week, and that there are so many girls that there's no way anyone can keep an eye on all of them, and so many suspects, it's impossible to figure out who might be guilty."

I nodded. That made sense. "I can understand why Fuentes doesn't want to believe that."

"Oh, sure. Can't blame him at all for that."

We sat in silence another minute.

"Can I ask you a question now?" Ty said.

"Sure."

He tilted his head. "Are you really a virgin?"

"Oh." I blushed. Not the question I'd been expecting, but... "Yeah. They checked at the clinic this morning."

"Why?"

I'd been asked that question before. Usually it came with a heavy dose of 'how can someone live to twenty-one without having sex,' or 'but you don't look like a hag.'

This time he just sounded interested. If he judged me, I couldn't hear it in his voice. So I told him the truth.

"I guess I never met anyone who wanted to be my first. Or anyone I wanted to be my first."

He nodded.

I added, "I've never really had a boyfriend. And I'm not

the type who goes to parties and picks up strangers."

"So when you asked me to come upstairs that first night..."

Oh. Um... "I was a little bit tipsy. And Mackenzie said that we all needed to get laid while we were here on spring break. But mostly it was because I liked you."

"Enough to sleep with me an hour after we met?"

"I would have probably chickened out," I admitted. "I wasn't quite drunk enough for that."

That made him smile. "Just as well I couldn't take you up on it, then."

I nodded.

He twirled his glass around watching the wine swirl. "But for the record..."

"Yes?"

"If I hadn't been working, I would have been tempted to say yes. Even if I don't usually jump into bed with girls I just met."

"Thank you."

He shrugged. "I guess I just... wanted you to know the truth. I said I lied about everything, but I didn't lie about that. I really do like you. And if I hadn't been here on duty, and you hadn't been in the middle of my investigation, I would have liked to spend more time with you."

That would have sounded better if it hadn't been for all those 'ifs.' "But now you can't?"

He shook his head. "Distractions aren't a good thing right now. If I take the night off, another girl will probably get grabbed tonight. And it'll be on my head."

And mine too, if I kept him with me.

Not that I thought I stood a chance of doing that. He'd be out there tonight, keeping an eye on things, whether I wanted him to be or not.

It made me like him even more. He put his own wants aside for the greater good, and what's not to like about that?

It was practically heroic, wasn't it?

We didn't talk about anything important again until

dinner was over and he was walking me home—back out to the lobby. "So if this guy seems to be focused on me," I said, "and you said earlier that he was, right?"

Ty nodded. "Seems to be, yeah."

"What'll happen when I'm not out there somewhere tonight?"

He shrugged. "I guess we'll find out. Hopefully he'll decide to wait for you instead of grabbing someone else."

"That wasn't what happened yesterday."

He didn't say anything to that, and I added, "If he doesn't see me tonight, will he take another girl and beat her up, too?"

"I don't know," Ty said, his voice tight.

"Should I go out and show myself, so he doesn't?"

"No. Absolutely not."

I must have looked undecided, because he added, "Please, Cassie. I can't do my job and worry about you at the same time. If you're out there, I'll only be able to concentrate on that."

That was rather flattering, to be honest, and it gave me the inkling of an idea...

But before I could grab it and take a better look at it, he'd put his hands on my shoulders and continued. "Please stay here tonight and let me watch out for other people."

Those green eyes looking down at me were the color of emeralds. I opened my mouth to tell him OK, I'd stay at the hotel and let him do his job, but I couldn't get my voice to cooperate. I just stood there, staring up at him, caught like a rabbit in a searchlight.

It looked like he hesitated for a second, but then he bent his head and brushed his lips over mine.

It wasn't much of a kiss. Just a quick touch, light and undemanding. Gone almost as soon as I realized it was happening.

I could feel it all the way down to my toes.

And he knew it, too. When he saw the look on my face, his lips curved. His hands moved from my shoulders up to my cheeks, and then he kissed me again.

And kept on kissing me. Until my head swam and my knees shook and I had to grab fistfuls of his shirt so I wouldn't melt into a puddle on the floor in front of him.

Finally he leaned his forehead against mine and closed his eyes. "Please stay inside tonight, Cassie."

His voice was husky.

I nodded. I couldn't speak.

"Thank you."

He gave me one last kiss, this one on the tip of my nose, and straightened.

"Will I see you tomorrow?" I asked.

He hesitated. "What were you planning to do tomorrow?"

"More sightseeing."

He didn't answer, and I added, "I can't stay in my room for the rest of spring break, Ty. I won't. This may be my only chance to see Key West. I want to enjoy it."

He nodded. "I'll pick you up at ten."

"Really?" He'd spend the day with me?

"I don't think anything's gonna happen to you during the day. But I don't think anything's gonna happen to anyone else, either. And I'd rather stick with you."

"I'd rather stick with you too," I said, and watched him walk out before I took the elevator up to my room.

CHAPTER *Ten*

Sightseeing was more fun with Ty than alone. It's always nicer when you have someone to share stuff with. I guess maybe that was Mackenzie's reasoning behind her demand that we not see much of each other this week: without girlfriends, we'd be forced to find other company.

Ty was great company. We even ended up taking a trolley tour, although not a haunted one. During the day, the trolley was cheerful and red, and did sightseeing tours. It did point out a few of the supposedly haunted houses that Carmen had mentioned the other night, though: the Audubon House, the Marrero Guest Mansion—where the owner's widow, the beautiful Enriquetta, was kicked out and left to live on the streets—and the Hard Rock Café. And of course it took us past Sloppy Joe's Bar and Captain Tony's and several other more or less well-known establishments.

Augustus and Jehosephat were just Jeff and Arthur today, out of their ghostly costumes and makeup. Nothing scary about them. Although Jeff's eyes lingered on my legs when I climbed into the trolley. "He gives me the creeps," I muttered to Ty when we sat down.

He grinned. "I hate to tell you, Cassie, but I look at your legs, too."

"You don't drool."

"I try not to." He winked.

I was wearing shorts, because it was warm and I wanted to be comfortable. But as I caught Jeff glancing at me in the rearview mirror again, I wished I'd gone with the jeans.

"You don't think he...? Or both of them?"

Ty shook his head. "Profiling says single individual, not a team. So chances are not. But I'll have Fuentes check his background—both of their backgrounds—if he hasn't already."

I nodded. "What about the guy at your motel? The one who reads the cartoon porn?"

"Already cleared. He worked the late shift Sunday night."

"So you thought he was creepy, too?"

He shrugged. "I'd rather investigate a lot of innocent people than miss the asshole who's doing this because I'm too afraid to do my job."

Right.

"Did anything happen last night?"

"Not that we've heard about," Ty said, looking like he was waiting for the other shoe to drop.

"No new victims?"

"None we've found."

"Is that good?"

"It's good that another girl wasn't raped. But it doesn't get us any closer to catching this creep." He made a frustrated sound and shoved his fingers into his hair. "He may have gone underground. Maybe beating up that girl on Tuesday night changed something for him, and he's done for this year."

I nodded sympathetically. It was your classic Catch-22. Of course nobody wanted another girl to be assaulted, but unless something happened, there was no way to figure out who the guy was and to catch him. So far, he'd left precious few clues.

"I was thinking last night," I told Ty as the trolley made its way through the streets and Jeff's voice droned over the speakers.

"Yeah?"

"You said yesterday that it looks like this guy has focused on me. The first victim was a blonde in a pink dress, on a night when I was a blonde in a pink dress. And the second victim was assaulted in the cemetery, after you and I had walked through the cemetery."

He nodded.

"On Tuesday night, I was drugged, but I got away. And another girl—another blonde—was beaten and I assume raped."

He nodded.

"On Sunday and Monday, you walked me home, so he couldn't get at me. On Tuesday, I got away from him. I have no idea how, but I must have."

He nodded.

"But I'm nothing special."

"I wouldn't say that," Ty murmured, with a look that made my heart skip a beat and then start staggering.

I forced myself to sound calm. "You know what I mean. I'm OK-looking, but I'm not especially pretty. Or sexy. There are a lot of prettier girls. And I haven't done anything to catch anyone's attention." Like dancing on the bar or pulling my top off so everyone could see my breasts. And yes, that had happened.

He shook his head.

"So I thought... is it possible that he singled me out not because of me, but because of you?"

He blinked.

"I'm nobody. But you're somebody. You're the FBI agent the Key West police called in to catch this guy. And you talked to me on Sunday night in Captain Crow's. Nothing had happened yet then. But that night, another blonde in a pink dress was raped."

"Damn," Ty said softly. I imagined he was probably thinking it through and seeing what I was seeing—or thought I was seeing—but I kept talking just in case.

"So is it possible that if you'd talked to a brunette that night—if you'd talked to Quinn—it would be brunettes with long, straight hair who were getting raped?"

"Fuck."

"What I mean is, did this guy pick me to focus on because you focused on me?"

"Fuck. Shit. Damn." His voice was flat, so lacking in emotion I knew he had to be seething. "I can't believe I didn't think of that."

I'd take that as a yes. "Did you test that glass you took away from me that first night?"

He nodded.

"Was there anything in it?"

"Nothing that shouldn't be. You'd had your back to it for a while, so I took it away just to be safe. But nobody tried to drug you that night. Damn." He started his litany of curses again. I left him to it.

He was still cursing when the trolley pulled up outside the East Martello Fort Museum, home of Robert the Doll.

It was a big brick building that looked like—and once was—a fort. "Constructed during the Civil War by the U.S. Army," Jeff said as we all made our way out of the trolley and into the parking lot, "to protect Key West against a potential Confederate sea assault. It was abandoned in its unfinished state by the end of the war. It was used for Army and Navy training during World War Two, and in 1950, the Key West Historical Society opened it as a museum. We'll spend forty five minutes here. If you want to take a picture of Robert the Doll, remember to ask nicely."

He grinned. Most of the others glanced at him over their shoulders as they trudged toward the entrance to the museum. He caught my eye and winked.

Ty was still bent over his phone, texting furiously. I guess he was communicating silently with Detective Fuentes, telling him our new theory. It was so obvious to me I couldn't believe no one had thought of it, but it seemed they hadn't.

"Are you coming in?" I asked when his thumbs stopped moving.

He looked up and around, like he wasn't quite sure where we were. Then his eyes cleared. "Sure. Wouldn't want you to tackle Robert on your own."

"I don't plan to tackle him." In fact, I didn't plan to have anything to do with him at all. I might not even approach him. My own life was creepy enough just now, thank you very much; I didn't need any help from ghosts or haunted dolls.

"I'll keep you safe," Ty said, taking my hand.

He did. As we walked through cavernous rooms filled with things like Talbott Jehosephat Windsor's bone cart and a life-size wax replica of Karl Tanzler working on Elena's corpse, I was very glad for the warmth of his hand and the solidness of his body next to me. It was chilly in the old stone rooms, and the creepy displays added their own sort of psychological chill to the physical one.

Robert the Doll resided in a glass case in front of a wall full of letters from all over the world apologizing for being rude to him.

He was big, much bigger than I'd realized. The size of a small child. He was dressed in a sailor suit with some sort of plush animal on his lap, a dog or a lion, and his face was at the same time vacant and strangely expressive, with brown button eyes.

"Want his picture?" Ty asked in my ear.

I shook my head.

"He might be offended if you don't at least ask."

He's a doll!

But I didn't say it out loud. Wouldn't want Robert to hear.

"Fine." I took a breath. "Robert? You look very nice. Would it be OK if we took your picture?"

We waited. Nothing happened.

"No thunderbolts," I told Ty under my breath.

"Wait. Look." He nodded to the doll.

I peered into the glass case again. It was probably my imagination, but it looked like Robert was leaning just a fraction of an inch farther left.

"Better hurry, before he changes his mind," Ty said and lifted his phone.

He snapped a picture. "Tell him thanks."

I dredged up a smile. "Thank you, Robert."

I can't swear to it, but it looked like Robert smiled too.

He's a doll. He's just a doll.

I admit it. I walked backward away from the glass box. Like you would with royalty, or with a growling Rottweiler you didn't want to turn your back on. I wasn't exactly sure which category applied to this situation, but in either case, it seemed like a good idea.

"Looks like Robert likes leggy blondes, too," Ty said when we were outside.

I shot him a look. "A shame we can't pin the assaults on him."

"Don't let him hear you say that," Ty said. "That's what started this whole mess, you know. Whenever Eugene Otto got in trouble, he'd blame Robert. No wonder Robert got tired of it."

Whatever. "Were you texting Detective Fuentes?"

He nodded. "He thinks we may be onto something. It would explain a lot."

Yes, it would.

"And he's not very happy."

"Because if we're right, it means this would have to be someone who knows who you are. Right?"

He nodded, his mouth set on grim. "That's right."

"So someone local." Which naturally wouldn't make Fuentes happy, when he'd kept his fingers crossed for a visitor.

"Not just a local," Ty said, "but one of a fairly small group of locals. The ones who were notified I was here."

"Who's that?"

He sighed. "Let's walk. We have fifteen minutes until the trolley leaves. You wanna climb to the top of the tower?"

"Sure," I said. "The top of the tower sounds good."

"The view's nice." He took my hand again and pulled me across the grass. The blades tickled my bare legs.

Once we were on top of the lookout tower—where the view *was* nice; all blue ocean and blue sky and fluffy, white clouds—he continued. "Fuentes was the one who wanted to call in the FBI. He talked the brass into it. When I got here, they had me stand up in front of the entire police force and give a profile of the guy. The behavioral unit at Quantico put it together for me. They said he's young, 20-30, probably white—since all the victims have been young and white—keeps to himself, a loner, socially backward, and a local... although I didn't mention that last part when I presented the profile."

"But the behavioral unit said he was local?"

"They said he most likely was," Ty said, leaning his arms on the parapet and gazing out to sea. "I thought it would be better if I didn't say anything about it."

Probably so. I leaned my arms on the warm stone next to him. "So the entire police force knows who you are. Who else?"

"The cops had to know, so they could help me if I needed it. The mayor knows, of course. The rest of the city government. And after that, they called a meeting of every bar and restaurant owner in Key West. Everyone who owns a place where they serve drinks. That includes most of the hotel people, too."

"That's a lot of people."

He nodded. "But compared to the population as a whole—not to mention the students on spring break—it's a pretty small group. Less than two hundred people altogether."

"That isn't small." Not when we were looking for a single guy.

Ty shrugged. "If we're right and someone targeted you

because of me, it's one of that group. Someone Fuentes knows. Someone he trusted with the truth. So obviously he's upset."

I bit my lip. "We could be wrong."

"Yeah," Ty said, "but I don't think we are."

Below us, the rest of the trolley passengers began straggling out of the museum. Jeff crossed the parking lot in the direction of the bus. The sun shone on the balding top of his head.

"What about him?" I asked. "Would he know who you are?"

"Depends on who he's been talking to," Ty said. "I wouldn't doubt it." He turned toward the stairs. "Let's go. We don't wanna be left behind." He headed across the top of the tower. I took a last look at the view and followed.

"You do realize," I told him after the tour was over, as we were walking up Duval Street from the trolley, "that with what we know, there's a very easy way you can catch this guy."

He looked at me. Not like he didn't know what I was talking about, but like he didn't want to think about it. Or hear about it. Or talk about it.

I ignored it. "If he wants me, you can give him me. And then catch him in the act."

"You've lost your mind," Ty said.

"No, I haven't. It makes perfect sense. You said it yourself. He might have gone underground. He didn't grab another girl last night. He might not grab one tonight. He can obviously control himself, if he only does this during spring break."

"There's probably something about spring break that sets him off. Something happened to him during spring break, something traumatic. Or maybe he just doesn't like all the strangers invading his town."

I shrugged. As far as I could see, it didn't matter what the creep's reasoning was. "If he wants me, but he can't have me, he may lay low until next year. And then you'll have to start all over again. But if we lure him out tonight—"

He shot me a blistering look. “No fucking way!”

“It makes sense.”

“I don’t care if it makes sense,” Ty snarled, “I’m not letting you go out tonight to try to lure a rapist. No. And that’s final.”

I pulled my hand out of his and stopped in the middle of the sidewalk with my hands on my hips. “You do realize you can’t tell me what to do, right?”

He stopped too, to stare at me. “I damn well can.”

“Only if I let you,” I said. “If I want to go out tonight and get drunk and get myself in trouble, you can’t stop me.”

“Watch me!”

This really wasn’t going well. I took my hands off my hips and lifted them to his cheeks. “Ty.”

His jaw was clenched. And when he lifted his own hands and wrapped them around my wrists, I could feel the effort it took for him to stay calm. “Yeah.”

“I know you want me to be safe. And I appreciate it. But I want you to catch this guy. I don’t want anyone else getting raped, especially not on my account.”

He opened his mouth, and I added, before he had a chance to speak. “I’ll wear a wire. Or whatever it is they do on TV.”

His lips twitched. “It’s an earbud now. No wires.”

“Earbud, then. I’ll wear an earbud. And keep my phone on. And be very, very careful.”

“This isn’t TV, Cassie.”

“I know that. But if I do this, and he takes the bait, you can close this case tonight.” And be off duty tomorrow. In time for the last day of my spring break.

“Maybe Carmen...” Ty began, and I shook my head.

“It has to be me. Carmen is Detective Fuentes’s sister, and if this guy is local, he knows that. For you to suddenly start focusing your attention on Carmen would be a dead giveaway that you’re onto him. And if he wants blondes, he’s not going to go for Carmen, anyway.”

“It would piss Fuentes off if he went after Carmen.”

Sure. But— “I don’t think this is about Fuentes. I think it’s about you. And you've been paying attention to me."

"I can start paying attention to Carmen."

"Not in time for tonight," I said.

"It doesn't have to be tonight."

"Yes, it does. If we fail tonight, we'll have another chance tomorrow. If we don't try tonight, and fail tomorrow, we won't have another chance at all. I'm going home Saturday morning."

He was quiet after that. I pressed my advantage.

"Can we at least talk about it? Without you yelling at me? And not in the middle of the street?"

"Yeah," Ty said, taking my hand again. "Let's go talk about it."

He towed me up the road.

CHAPTER *Eleven*

Captain Crow's was hopping.

I'd have thought that maybe, after almost a week of partying, people might have gotten tired of getting drunk and getting laid, but no. The spring break party showed no signs of abating. If anything, it was going stronger. People were looking at having to go home in two days, I guess, and trying to make the most of the time they had left.

Hopefully that would occur to our rapist too, and he'd realize that in two days, his supply of prey would dry up. It was a hell of a thing to wish for—that someone would decide the time was ripe to rape again; and to rape me!—but it was the only way I could think of to catch him.

I recognized quite a few of the people I'd seen here the first night, and a few of the nights since. Stan the cop had been and gone, enjoying another glass of Coke at the bar, while Carmen was still sitting where he'd left her, in a shirt that said *Keep Off the Dunes*. She kept glancing at Ty, across the table from me, but he pretended he didn't notice.

The Ivy League Dudes were here as usual, knocking back shots of Tequila. At the rate they were going, I'd have thought they'd have worked their way through Captain Crow's stash by now and been forced to move on to another bar, but no.

Quinn's guy was with them, and so was Quinn. She looked uncomfortable, and I couldn't blame her. As the evening went on, they acted more and more like hyenas.

James wasn't as bad as the others, at least from where I was sitting, but his friends did their best to goad him into joining them. After a while Quinn got up, either to get herself a new drink, or to talk to the bartender about having them cut off. Or maybe just because she needed a break from the bastards.

She stopped on her way across the floor to give me a hug, and assured me that yes, although the rest of the Ivy League Dudes were obnoxious, James was OK and she liked him. I reminded her not to accept any drinks from strangers—especially not from the group she was with, although I didn't say that specifically—and she rolled her eyes before she moved on to the bar.

Barry wasn't working today; it was Mackenzie's guy, Austin, behind the bar. I hadn't really had a chance to talk to him yet, had just seen him from a distance, but he must know who Quinn was, because he greeted her with a smile and a wink.

James's face turned to stone, though, so obviously he didn't appreciate her talking to—smiling at, maybe even flirting with—another guy. It looked like his friends were getting on him about it, too, until he shot something back that made them all shut up and gape at him.

By then, Quinn had made it almost all the way back. I saw her hesitate just beyond their table. Probably able to hear what they were talking about, but they hadn't noticed her yet. I was too far away to hear what they were saying, but I could see them wrestling over something.

I squinted. Small and white and crumpled...

Paper?

No, fabric. Small and white and...

Surely that wasn't someone's underwear? Was it?

I saw Quinn freeze, and then she squared her shoulders and gave them what-for, before she marched out, her face pale. Ivy League Dude—James—tried to grab her arm, but she shook him off like a bug, like she couldn't stand to have him touch her.

There was a moment of silence, and then someone cracked a joke that made them all howl with laughter. All except James. He was still staring at the door where Quinn had disappeared. For a second, I thought maybe he'd man up and go after her, but no. He relaxed back into the chair, smiling at the rest of the jackasses he was with. The smile looked a little forced, admittedly, but he was smiling, the jerk.

"Excuse me."

I was halfway up from the table when Ty grabbed my wrist. His voice was low. "Where are you going?"

Wasn't it obvious? "I'll be right back. Two minutes."

I twitched out of his grasp and headed for the door. He must have allowed it, because I imagine I wouldn't have been able to shake him otherwise. He was probably trained to hold on to people.

By the time I got outside, Quinn was halfway down the block. I had to run to catch up, and then I had to stop her from trying to fight me off before she realized I was me and not His Effing Majesty, Ivy League Dude.

I swung her around to face me. "What happened? Are you OK?"

She looked awful, with teardrops hanging in her lashes. Her voice caught when she told me, "He made a bet, Cass. A bet to get me into bed."

"I'll kill him." Or ask Ty to kill him. He was an FBI agent; he was probably armed. "Wait here and I'll be right back."

"No," Quinn managed, with something halfway between a sob and a choked laugh, "he's not worth it." She dashed a hand over her face. "Oh, God, I'm a mess. And there's more. His stupid friend blabbed about Mac to the press. The paparazzi are swarming her right now—Austin tipped me off. Mac probably thinks he did it, but it was James. Did you know about this?"

I shook my head. "No, I haven't heard anything." I'd had my own problems to deal with. God, I didn't need this right now. Not on top of everything else. "What should we do?"

"I'm going up to her room. Austin said she was holed up."

I glanced over my shoulder at the door to the bar. "D'you want me to come with you?" *Please say no.*

I mean, I would go if she said yes. Mackenzie was my friend, and if she needed me—if Quinn needed me—I'd totally be there. For either of them. Both of them.

But Ty was waiting. And he counted on me. Even if he didn't want to admit it.

"No," Quinn said. "Stay. I don't think Mac needs both of us swooping in if she's trying to lay low. And I need some time to process."

That made sense. And got me off the hook. But still... "I don't know... I hate leaving both of you alone when all this stuff is going on."

She squeezed my hands. "Cassie, go back to the bar. For God's sakes, one of us has to have a good wrap-up to this week. I'll check in with Mac and we'll be fine. Text us later."

"Are you sure?"

She nodded. "I'm sure."

"OK. But tell her I'm thinking about her. All right?"

She promised she would, and we went our separate ways: Quinn to play hide-and-seek with the paparazzi, and me to play hide-and-seek with a rapist.

When I got back inside the bar, things looked much the same as when I'd left. Carmen was still at the bar, Ty was still alone at our table, and the Ivy League Dudes were whooping it up in the back.

"Are you armed?" I asked Ty when I slid onto my seat across from him.

He stared at me blankly.

"Because I'd really like to shoot them all."

His lips curved, but he said, "That wouldn't be a good idea."

"I know. But I still want to. Do you you know what he did?"

He shook his head.

"Made a bet that he could take her to bed. The bastard."

I scowled at Ivy League Dude—just at the time when he looked around and saw me. I did my best to convey wordlessly exactly what kind of lowlife I thought he was, and it must have worked, because he looked guilty. About a minute later, he left. Maybe he was hoping to plead his case with Quinn, although he may just have had enough of his friends. I knew I had.

"I'd really like it if it was one of them," I told Ty.

He glanced at them. "Could be one of them. Obnoxious rich kids. Used to doing whatever they want and getting away with it."

"That's what I thought."

"Maybe you should switch from English Lit to psychology."

He took a sip of his drink. We were both drinking Sprite with a lime wedge, fake vodka tonic. No real alcohol tonight.

"I don't think so," I said. "I like escaping into a good book."

He shrugged. "There's something to be said for making a difference in the real world."

Maybe so. I made an effort to push Quinn and Ivy League Dude and Mackenzie and the paparazzi from my mind. Just for tonight. I had my own problems to focus on tonight.

Ty must be thinking the same thing, because he told me, "I really wish you'd change your mind about this, Cassie."

"It's too late," I said.

His eyes were intense. "No, it isn't. I can take you back to the hotel right now."

"And wait while he finds someone else to assault."

He didn't say anything to that.

"No," I said. "If we're right, it's already too late. He didn't grab anyone else last night, because he didn't see me. But I'm out here tonight. He'll try for me before he'll go for anyone else." If we were right.

"I don't like it," Ty said, talking to his drink.

"I know." I wasn't looking forward to it either. I just didn't see any other way to fix the situation. Letting the guy crawl back into his hole for another year wasn't a possibility. Not when we had a chance to flush him out. We should take it. Even if the thought made me feel like I wanted to throw up.

"What if something goes wrong?" Ty said.

"Then..." I'd get drugged again, and probably raped this time too. Maybe beaten up. But I'd survive. The other girls had survived; I would too.

And anyway, that wouldn't happen.

I shook my head. "Nothing's going to go wrong."

"What if it does?"

"You'll make sure it doesn't."

His hands tightened around the glass. "What if I fail?"

"You won't."

"Easy for you to say."

No, it wasn't. If he failed, it was my safety on the line. We both knew it.

"It'll be OK," I said. "Fuentes knows, right?"

He nodded.

"And he's got extra cops on the streets."

"They don't know to keep an eye on you specifically, though. Just to keep an eye out in general."

I tilted my head to look at him. "How did he take it when you asked him not to tell anyone else? He must have realized why, right?"

"He's not stupid," Ty said. "He knew exactly why. And he wasn't happy about it. He doesn't want it to be someone he knows. But he understands. And he'll be out there watching you."

Good.

I glanced at my watch. Ten to ten. A few minutes early,

but— "Can we get started, do you think?"

"Nervous?"

I nodded.

"Are you sure you don't want me to—?"

"Yes!" I pushed my chair back hard enough that it toppled. "Dammit, Ty, stop asking me that!"

"Cassie..."

"No! Just... shut up!"

I swirled on my heel and headed for the bathroom before anyone could look at me too closely and see that the anger on my face was mostly feigned. But we had to stage an argument, a reason for me to leave Captain Crow's on my own, without Ty, and this lead-in would serve as well as any other.

Lots of people were staring at me as I made my way to the bathroom. That was a bit disconcerting, since I've never been happy about attracting that kind of attention. Mackenzie likes the limelight, at least when she's in the mood for adoration, but I don't.

We needed it, though. We needed a public argument and a very public parting of the ways.

I stayed in the restroom a few minutes—every second bringing me closer to the ten o'clock mark—before I went back out into the bar. The same eyes followed my progress back to the table.

Ty had righted my chair while I'd been gone, and he watched me warily, with obvious irritation. *Undercover*, I reminded myself. *Used to pretending.*

"What the hell, Cassie?" He pitched his voice low, like he was trying to be quiet, but loud enough that everyone who wanted to would be able to hear. "What's wrong with you?"

"I'm on spring break! I'm going home in two days! I just want to have a good time! Is that so much to ask?"

"Keep your fucking voice down!" Ty hissed, at the same time one of the Ivy League Dudes shouted that he'd show me a good time.

I ignored him, even as my cheeks burned and his friends

hooted with laughter. Instead I faced Ty across the table. "Maybe I should take him up on it."

"Do whatever the hell you want!" Ty said. "If you can't tell that I'm just trying to protect you..."

"I don't need you to protect me! I'm old enough to take care of myself!"

I was probably overacting—way too many exclamation points—but I was on a roll now. "I just want to have a good time. And you constantly telling me I 'shouldn't do this' and 'shouldn't go there' is ruining my vacation!"

"Then go wherever the hell you want. And if you get hurt, it'll be your own fault!"

"Thank you!" I said. "I'll do that!"

I swung on my heel and headed for the door.

"Goddamn fucking bitch!" Ty growled behind me. And then— "Cassie! Wait!"

I didn't. I pushed the door open and headed out into the night. Behind me, I could hear the scramble as Ty followed.

Ten seconds later, he burst through the door behind me. "Cassie! Dammit!"

I glanced over my shoulder at him, and ran.

He didn't follow, of course. Part of me wished he would, but I knew he couldn't. That wasn't part of the plan. He had to go back inside Captain Crow's and complain loudly about idiots who wouldn't listen to reason and girls who wouldn't put out. After a few minutes, Carmen would decide to keep him company, and they'd sit there and flirt and wait for word from Ricky Fuentes that everything had gone according to plan.

I, meanwhile, had my own job to do. After a block or so, I slowed down to a walk, while still shooting glances over my shoulder as if I were afraid—or hopeful—he might be coming.

Just in case someone was watching.

No one seemed to be. It was just business as usual on the streets of Key West. College students walking or staggering from bar to bar. Someone bent over a trash can on the street corner, either getting rid of the contents of their stomach or looking for cans. A couple of cars passed by, driving slowly. The ghost trolley pulled up alongside me and Jehosephat—Jeff, back in makeup and costume—nodded.

I forced a smile and kept going. He kept driving, while he entertained his passengers with the story of John James Audubon's time in Key West and whether the famous painter really was the dauphin of France. (He wasn't.)

On the next block I slowed down even more. There were fewer people here, as I got farther from the bars and restaurants on Duval Street, and closer to the cemetery. Another glance over my shoulder showed me that no one was following. Carmen had probably rescued Ty by now, and was flirting with him.

Hopefully he wouldn't get so caught up in it that he'd forget about me.

The entrance to the cemetery rose ahead, the whitewashed tombs and monuments behind the fence gleaming palely.

"Cassie?"

I must have jumped a foot, and my heart felt like it got lodged in my throat. It took a couple of seconds for me to swallow it, and my laugh was distinctly forced. "Stan. God, you scared me."

"Sorry." He stepped out of the shadows near the gate, teeth gleaming. "What are you doing?"

"Just walking." I shot another glance over my shoulder. Stan glanced that way, too.

"Alone?"

I nodded. "Ty was getting on my nerves, so I ditched him at Captain Crow's. He followed me outside, but I guess he got tired of trying to catch up."

Stan looked up the street again. "I don't see him."

"Me neither. But just in case, I think I'll cut through the cemetery." I took a couple steps toward the gates.

"You want me to go with you?" Stan asked, hand on his weapons belt.

I shook my head. "Thanks, but that's not necessary. I'm not

afraid of dead people."

And Ricky Fuentes must have stationed him here, so it was probably best if he stayed where he was supposed to stay.

Had Fuentes told him what was going on tonight, and that's why Stan was here?

He wasn't supposed to. Per the plan, it was supposed to be just Fuentes, Ty, Carmen and me in the know.

So maybe this was Stan's regular beat. I'd seen him here once before, too, after all.

I decided I couldn't assume anything. I certainly couldn't assume he knew what was going on, beyond doing his usual job. So I said, "See you," and ducked through the gates into the cemetery itself. Stan looked up and down the street and faded back into the shadows under a big tree near the entrance.

I walked into the maze of tombs and headstones and monuments on my own, more slowly now.

The place looked exactly as it had two nights ago, big and creepy, with the whitewashed stone shining palely, like bone.

I had told Stan the truth. I'm not afraid of dead people. And I don't believe in ghosts. But walking along the shadowy paths between the graves, trying to listen for sounds above the rustling of the palm trees, was still pretty creepy. I had something scarier than a ghost waiting for me, after all.

Unless we were wrong. Unless the girl on Tuesday night had been the swan song, and our guy was done for the year.

Or unless I wasn't his target. If Ty was this guy's focus, then any girl Ty paid attention to would become a focus too. If he stopped paying attention to me, maybe I'd stop being a target. I could wander around the cemetery all night, while our guy was on the other side of town, raping someone else.

Like Carmen.

If any girl Ty paid attention to became the target, then Carmen was the one in danger tonight, not me.

There was a sound behind me, and I stopped and glanced over my shoulder.

Nothing there.

Or nothing I could see.

That meant either ghost, or someone who didn't want to be seen.

Detective Fuentes was here somewhere; maybe he'd just wanted to let me know he was keeping an eye on me.

I kept moving forward, keeping an ear out.

We had chosen this place deliberately, both for its convenient location and for its many, many hiding places. And also because the guy we were looking for had used it once before, successfully. According to Ty, he was probably comfortable here, and it held good memories for him.

Somehow, the thought of that was more chilling than the fact that I was walking alone through a cemetery at night, looking for a rapist.

There was another sound behind me, closer this time.

I swung on my heel and gasped as a tall figure loomed up in front of me.

CHAPTER *Twelve*

"You shouldn't be here alone," Stan said, and I let my breath out on another unconvincing laugh.

"I'm fine. Really."

He shook his head. "This isn't a good place at night. It's haunted, you know."

"I don't believe in ghosts," I said.

He shrugged. "I'll walk you through and out on the other side."

"You really don't have to..."

"It's my job," Stan said seriously. "To serve and protect paradise."

Like the logos on the squad cars. It was probably part of their oath, as well.

I glanced around, but there was no way around it that I could see. If he didn't know what was going on—and Fuentes wasn't supposed to have told him anything about it—he really was just doing his job. Making a fuss would only make him wonder why I was so determined to walk around in a graveyard alone at night.

It would probably be better to let him escort me through the cemetery, and then sneak back in through one of the other entrances once he was gone.

And Detective Fuentes was lying in wait somewhere. Maybe he'd see us and intercept Stan before he ruined everything. Nobody was likely to approach me while I was accompanied by a uniformed cop. If this took too long, the guy we were after might decide I was a lost cause again, and find someone else to rape.

If he was here, and wasn't busy watching Ty and Carmen, biding his time before he snatched a girl none of us were worried about.

"Did Connor show you all the graves the other night?" Stan asked after we had walked a couple of yards.

"Most of them, I think. The ones he thought I'd find interesting."

I looked around, distracted. Where the hell was Fuentes? Why didn't he come out of hiding and order Stan off of me so we could get back to the program?

"He isn't local, though," Stan said, "so he probably doesn't know all the stories."

"Probably not." There was no sign of Fuentes. But it was a big cemetery, and he might not have noticed me—noticed us—yet. I turned my attention back to Stan. "Did you grow up here?"

He nodded. "Saltwater Conch." There was pride in his voice.

"I don't know what that means," I admitted.

"Saltwater Conchs are natives of Key West. Freshwater Conchs have lived here for at least seven years."

"What about the people who've arrived within the last seven years?"

"They're nobody," Stan said with a shrug.

Uh-huh. "Why conchs?"

"White," Stan said. "The native Bahamians called the white

settlers 'conchs.' "

"After the big shells with the pink insides?"

He nodded.

"That's interesting. So do you like living here?"

"It's home," Stan said.

"It's a beautiful place. I'm glad I got to see it." I might even be back, although probably not for spring break. Once was enough.

"It's nicer when the streets aren't crawling with drunk college kids," Stan said.

Probably. Although I was one of those college kids, so he could have been a little more polite.

"I bet they—we—bring in a lot of revenue, though."

That's what Stan had said, wasn't it? In Captain Tony's the other night? That the mayor and the Chamber of Commerce and the local businesses hadn't been willing to consider canceling spring break because of the money. That a few rapes were worth it if it kept the revenue coming in.

Stan shrugged, and we walked forward in silence again, the only sound our footsteps scuffing along the ground. We were probably getting close to the middle of the cemetery by now. Ty had told me it was almost 20 acres, with a hundred thousand burials: many more than the current population of Key West. There wasn't a sound to be heard, other than our own breathing.

"Water?" Stan held out a bottle without looking at me.

"Thanks." I took it and was about to screw off the cap when I realized what I was doing. "You know, never mind. I had a lot to drink at Captain Crow's. I need a bathroom more than I need water right now."

I tried to hand it back while I looked around. *Dammit, Fuentes, where are you?*

Stan didn't take it. "Then you need to rehydrate," he said.

My heart gave a slow, hard thud, and then another. I tried to keep my voice steady. "I really don't, you know."

He stopped. "Drink the water, Cassie."

"That's what you said last time, too. Isn't it?"

He smiled, and the light glinted on his teeth. "You weren't supposed to remember that."

I tightened my hand on the bottle and felt the plastic crinkle. "I didn't, really. I thought it might have been a dream."

"No," Stan said. "Not a dream."

Obviously not. I wondered how it had escaped me before how big he was. It was probably because he'd never stood so close, and had never leaned over me before. I'd seen him from a distance, on the beach and outside the cemetery, but in the bar, he'd been sitting down.

I cleared my throat and thought about screaming. Fuentes might be near enough to hear me, although twenty acres is a bit of ground to cover. And if I screamed, Stan would probably shut me up right away. In a way that might leave me with no second chance to scream.

No, better to keep him talking for as long as I could. Maybe Fuentes would find us.

Unless Stan knew exactly what was going on, and had already dealt with Fuentes.

A chill ran down my spine. Fuentes could be lying unconscious behind a tomb right now.

Or worse, dead.

He might be in no position to come to my aid.

I could ask, but if Stan didn't know what was going on, and had only taken the bait we'd dangled in front of him, I certainly didn't want to tip him that Fuentes was nearby.

"So..." I said instead, "it was you?"

"Of course."

"All of them? All the girls?"

He nodded.

"Why?"

"Because they come here," Stan said, "to *my* town, and they foul it up. They drink, and they puke, and they whore."

"Couldn't you just arrest them? Raping them doesn't solve anything."

"They ask for it," Stan said. "With their drinking and whoring ways."

I blinked. "I don't have drinking and whoring ways." I had the least whoring ways of anyone I knew. "The others didn't either. They were virgins. All of them."

Elizabeth and Jeanine and the poor battered girl in the hospital, whatever her name was.

"They shouldn't be out here," Stan said, "putting themselves on display."

"I didn't put myself on display!"

"That was last year," Stan said. "This year is different."

My heart was knocking against my ribs, and it was hard to keep the conversation going when I was so scared. Ghosts are one thing, insanity another. And this guy clearly wasn't quite right in the head. He was standing here, calmly and reasonably explaining to me why it made sense that he'd raped five girls. My voice shook when I asked, "What's different this year?"

"Last year I chose the sluts," Stan said. "The ones who were asking for it. Like Carmen."

Carmen? "You raped Carmen?"

He chuckled. "Didn't know that, did you?"

I shook my head. "She's not here on spring break. She's a local. A Conch, like you. Why...?"

"She needed to learn a lesson," Stan said. "She was out there drinking and whoring, too. Spreading her legs for the college boys, but not giving any of us the time of day."

'Us' being the locals, I assumed. The Conchs.

"And it worked, too. She stopped being a slut after that."

"So you decided the same lesson would work for other girls."

He nodded. "It worked fine last year. Nobody paid any attention. But this year, Ricky Fuentes called in the FBI."

His face darkened and his fists clenched. Big fists, disproportionately large for his skinny frame. "A fucking FBI agent, straight out of college. Younger than me. And he takes charge and stands up there and says the guy we're looking for is young and white and can't get a date, and we all have to listen to him."

I could see why that would be galling. Especially if Stan had wanted a date—with Carmen, say. Carmen, who wouldn't give him the time of day.

"So this year..."

"This year I waited," Stan said. "I watched the FBI agent, and I waited. On Saturday, he didn't do nothing. Just sat around and watched. But on Sunday he talked to you. And I could tell he liked you."

So I'd been right. Stan had focused on me—on us blondes—because of Ty. Because Ty had focused on me. Nice to know I was right, even now.

For all the good it would do me.

C'mon, Fuentes!

I didn't look around, didn't dare do anything to tip Stan off that we might not be alone, but I broadcast my thoughts as far and as wide as I could.

"But he walked you home," Stan said, "so I couldn't get at you. Walked right by me and grinned, like he fucking knew!"

That's right: Ty had said hello to all the cops we'd passed that first night. I hadn't noticed Stan then, not until the next morning on the beach.

"So you picked someone else instead."

"Another blonde in a pink dress," Stan said. "Figured that'd rattle the bastard."

And it had, although Ty had hidden it well. "And the second night, he walked me through the cemetery. And you picked another girl and brought her here."

"I was here already," Stan said, "remember?"

Of course. He'd been standing outside the cemetery when I walked past on my way to Captain Crow's. But when Ty and I came back, he'd been gone.

"I almost grabbed you then," he told me. "You stopped to talk to me. But that fucking couple came out of the cemetery, and you ran off."

God. So close...

I swallowed. "And then the next night...?" He'd sat next to me at the bar, drinking his Coke and planning to rape me. And I'd had no idea.

"You left Captain Tony's alone," Stan said, his fists opening and closing.

I tightened my grip on the water bottle and sent out another silent hail. *Fuentes! Wake up, dammit!*

"I thought finally my luck had changed. You started walking with me, and I got the water into you. I was gonna leave you on his fucking doorstep!"

So that was why Ty had found us going in the opposite direction of my hotel. We were headed toward Richardson's.

"But then he caught up, and I had to pretend I'd found you like that and hope you didn't remember anything. And he won again!"

"So you went and found another girl."

"It was her own fault," Stan said. "I didn't have another dose of Special K on me, so I had to give her Roach instead. She didn't go under fast enough."

He might as well have been talking Greek, but I nodded like I understood. If I had the chance, I'd ask someone to explain later. At a guess, whatever Roach was, it didn't make someone as docile as whatever Special K was, and so the girl had fought. And in Stan's book, that made it her fault that he'd had to beat her into submission.

"But you didn't leave her in front of Richardson's."

"She wasn't you!" Stan snarled. "Now drink the goddamn water!"

"I don't want to drink the water."

His hand moved, I assumed toward the gun on his belt. I hurled the bottle at him as hard as I could, and took off running.

I didn't expect it to do any damage. It was just a soft plastic bottle, the kind that crinkled when I squeezed it. But I'd left the top mostly unscrewed, and when the bottle hit him in the chest, the top came off and water splashed everywhere. It distracted him for long enough that I was able to duck behind a box tomb, still close enough that I could hear him cursing.

I thought about moving on, but if I did, there was a good chance he'd see me scrambling across the ground, or at least that he'd hear me. I figured I was safer where I was, flat in the dirt in the shadow of the stone box.

That was until I realized that not only did he have a gun hanging from his belt, he had a flashlight, too.

The beam spilled across the grass a couple of yards in front of me, and I could hear him move, still muttering.

The flashlight beam came closer, and I heard his boots thump on the ground. I'm not sure he was even trying to move quietly. There was no point, since I could tell where he was by the light.

I held my breath and pushed my shoulder and hip against the cold stone of the box tomb as the light outlined the stone directly in front of me. Up one side, across the top, and down the other. Shades of *The Sound of Music*—that scene in the abbey where Rolf has the flashlight and the Von Trapp family is hiding.

"Come out, come out," Stan said with a giggle, "wherever you are."

Sounded like he was enjoying this a lot more than I was.

I made myself as small as I could when the beam reached the stone I was hiding behind. It passed in front of me, up the side of the box tomb, and skimmed over the top, along my back, before heading down the opposite side.

I bit my lip and squeezed my eyes shut. Don't make a sound. Don't make a sound. Don't...

"Found you!" He sounded gleeful, like a little kid playing hide-and-seek, leaning over the tomb and shining the light directly onto my head.

I screamed and tried to scramble away, but he vaulted the tomb—jumped right over it—and threw himself on top of me. I tried to scream again, but it's hard to do when someone who weighs seventy pounds more than you is sitting on your back.

"Looks like we're gonna have to do this the old-fashioned way," Stan said conversationally, "since you spilled my water."

Oh, God.

"No." I rocked back and forth, trying to dislodge him, but he didn't budge. I felt him fumble with something, and the next second, something cold poked at the back of my head.

"Stop," Stan said, "or I'll shoot you."

It's amazing the incentive a loaded gun pointed at your head can be. I stopped struggling, and lay still. *Dammit, Fuentes...*

"Don't worry." Stan chuckled. "This won't hurt a bit. Just lay back and think about Connor."

Sure. That'd help.

Although I would probably think about Ty. I already was.

God, he was going to be devastated tomorrow, wasn't he? And it was my own stupid fault. I hadn't caught on fast enough. If I had, I never would have allowed myself to be alone with Stan in a deserted place like this.

"Hands behind you," Stan said, grabbing my arms, and I felt the cold metal of a pair of handcuffs circle my wrists.

Great. That'd help in my getaway.

"OK. Up and over." He raised himself up far enough that he could flip me from my stomach onto my back. My cuffed hands were uncomfortable at the small of my back, but at least the ground was spongy and soft. It could have been worse, I guess. I could have been lying on pavement.

"Did you cuff all the others, too?" I asked breathlessly.

He chuckled. "Of course not. The others wanted it. They did everything I said to do. That's why they were out there drinking in the first place, dressed like hookers."

"I don't want it," I said.

"Sure you do. You wanted it on Sunday night. I saw the way you looked at Connor."

"I wanted it from him," I said. "I don't want it from you."

His face darkened. "You should have gotten it from him

while you had the chance. After this, he isn't gonna want you no more."

He dropped his hands and began fumbling with my zipper. I began screaming. And out of the darkness stepped a shadow that said, "Stan Laszlo, you are under arrest."

CHAPTER Thirteen

I spent Friday morning poolside, working on my tan. It was my last full day in Key West, and I'd neglected the tanning over the past couple of days.

That, and I just couldn't think of anything else to do. I had seen all of Key West I wanted to see; in fact, if it hadn't been for Ty—and Mackenzie and Quinn—I would have changed my ticket and gone home early.

Enrique Fuentes had come to my rescue just in time the night before, and had bundled me into a cab bound for the hotel, after calling Carmen and Ty to tell them what had gone down. I had stayed up for a while, hoping that Ty might stop by after they had finished talking to Stan, but either Stan had had more to say than I'd realized, or Ty hadn't wanted to stop by.

Part of me was worried I wouldn't see him again.

So when I looked up from my book just before noon and saw him standing in front of me, the relief was considerable.

"Hi." I smiled so widely he could probably see my wisdom

teeth.

"Hey." He grinned back. "Nice outfit."

Bikini. Not too big, but not too small, either. "Thanks." I blushed. "You too."

He was wearing jeans and another T-shirt. It was green today, like his eyes, with white letters. *Remember my name, you'll be screaming it later.*

I wanted to ask him whether that was intended to be a threat or a promise, or just an attempt to blend in with the college crowds, but before I could, he'd told me, "Go throw some clothes on. We're going to lunch."

"We are?"

He nodded. "Detective Fuentes and Carmen are waiting."

I definitely didn't want to miss that.

I got up from the lounge chair and gathered my stuff while Ty watched. Hopefully that was appreciation on his face, and not impatience. I turned to him. "D'you want to come upstairs while I change?"

He shook his head. "Better not. We don't wanna be late."

No, we didn't. And I guess it was sort of encouraging that he thought watching me change might make us late. Sounded like maybe the T-shirt had been trying to tell me something, after all.

I left him in the lobby while I headed upstairs in the elevator, to throw on a dress and a pair of sandals. I fluffed my hair, put on some lip-stuff and a pair of earrings, and went back down.

Fuentes and Carmen were waiting at I Dream of Wienie, a hot dog and Polish place in Old Town. Fuentes looked me up and down as I slid into the booth across from him. "Everything OK?"

"Fine." Maybe I should have been a basket case after last night, but the fact that Stan was safely behind bars had gone a long way toward making me sleep. I hadn't even had nightmares. "Nothing happened," I added.

"Plenty happened. It'd be understandable if you were a

little shaken up."

"I'm fine. Really. Just glad nobody else has to deal with him. He won't be going anywhere, right?"

Fuentes shook his head, biting into his dog. Ketchup and mustard decorated the corner of his mouth until he licked it away. "We've got enough evidence to put him away for a long time."

"He talked most of the night," Ty added, stirring a cup of coffee, his eyes on the spoon. I guess maybe he hadn't been to bed yet. Or if he had, not for long. "Times, places, details. Names we didn't have."

The bite of Polish curdled in my stomach and I put it down. "There were more girls? More than the ones we knew about?"

They both nodded, but it was Carmen who answered. "Including me."

I turned to her. "You didn't know...?" Hard to imagine someone being raped and not realizing it.

She shook her head. "It was a couple years ago. I was a lot wilder back then."

She slid a look at her brother, who nodded.

Carmen continued, "Spring break was a time for me to party, too. Free flow of alcohol, new out-of-town boy every night. Most of the time I didn't know who they were, and I often woke up alone. When I couldn't remember what happened, it was a lot like any other night."

"But instead of having too much to drink and sleeping with some out-of-town college boy, Stan drugged and raped you."

She nodded. "It's a good thing I've stopped drinking, or that woulda been a real wakeup call."

I could imagine. "I'm sorry."

For a second, something moved in her eyes, something a lot like pain, but then she shrugged. "I'd rather know."

"And it helps that he's behind bars," her brother added, with a strong snap of teeth.

Carmen nodded.

"So how many others did he name? How long has it been going on?" Longer than since last year, obviously, if Stan had raped Carmen a couple years ago.

"First time was four years ago," Fuentes said. "No name, and no police report at the time. No way of tracking the girl down now."

Gah.

"It was just the one girl that year, a crime of opportunity. No drugs involved, but he said the girl was drunk enough that he figured she'd have no idea who he was."

Double gah.

"The next year, he had figured out the drugs. It was three girls that year, including Carmen, but he lucked out and nobody reported being raped. He was probably pretty liberal with the doses, as he figured out what worked."

Ty grimaced, but didn't comment.

"And then last year, there were four. But only two realized what had happened and reported it. He couldn't use Rohypnol as much because of the dyes that had been added, so he moved to Ketamine."

"Special K?" I ventured.

Both Ty and Fuentes nodded. "Ketamine's what was in the water bottle last night," Fuentes said. "Very fast acting, but doesn't make you quite as unaware of what's going on. You're still mostly conscious, but you can't move."

"While roofies—Rohypnol, Roach—makes you forget everything," Ty added.

I looked from one to the other of them. "So what did he plan to do with me after he raped me? Since I would know who he was and could identify him?"

They exchanged a look, and for a second or two it looked like neither one of them wanted to answer.

"He didn't say," Ty said eventually, "but we figure he'd have ended up killing you. Like you said, you'd be able to identify him. He would want to prevent that."

"He planned to dump me on your doorstep, you know,"

I said, focused on keeping my voice steady. Not just rape, but murder? Looked like I'd gotten away even luckier than I'd originally thought. "You really pissed him off, coming here. Especially when you stood up and told everyone he couldn't get a date."

"He couldn't get a date," Carmen said. "I grew up with him, and he never had a girlfriend. Not sure whether that's because he was always a little odd, or whether he turned a little odd because he never could get a date."

Could go either way, I guessed.

I'd never had a boyfriend. Did that mean I was in danger of turning odd?

I glanced at Ty. The corner of his mouth tilted up. "Ready to go?" he asked me.

I nodded. "If you are."

"I'll walk you back to the hotel." He scooted out of the booth. I did the same. Ty and Detective Fuentes shook hands. Carmen gave me a hug and wished me well. I did the same for her. And then we walked out into the Key West sunshine.

"So you're leaving tomorrow," Ty said as we headed down the sidewalk hand in hand.

I nodded. "The flight's at eleven. I guess I have to be at the airport by ten. I'm meeting the others in the lobby at nine."

"Anything you wanted to do in Key West that you haven't had a chance to do? Snorkeling? Scuba diving?"

"I was hoping to have sex," I said.

He shot me a look. "You sure you still wanna do that? After last night?"

"I don't want to have sex with Stan." *I want to have sex with you.*

We walked in silence a few steps. His hand was warm and hard around mine.

"I think it would help," I added. "Until now, my only experience with sex has been this creepy guy planning to rape me. And if I leave Key West like this, that'll be what I'll take home with me."

He smiled crookedly. "So I'd be doing you a favor by taking you to bed? Improving your mental health?"

I flushed. "Something like that, I guess."

We walked another few feet.

"It isn't that I don't want to," Ty said.

"But?" There was definitely a 'but' at the end of that sentence, even if he hadn't said it. And this time it wasn't that he was working and I was part of his investigation.

"I wanna make sure it's really what you want. That I'm not taking advantage of you."

"You wouldn't be taking advantage of me. It's what I want." After last night, especially. "I want my first time to be with someone I choose, not someone who decides to rape me because he can."

Another half block passed before he spoke again. "Are you sure? About me?"

Very.

But before I had the chance to say so, he'd added, "You only get one chance at this, you know. Are you sure you want your first time to be with me?"

I slanted him a look. "Are you telling me I shouldn't?"

He smiled, but shook his head. "I don't want you to regret it. Giving your virginity to some guy you met on vacation, that you may not ever see again..."

I didn't want to think about that. "I'm sure," I said. "I'd like it to be you. If you wouldn't mind."

"No," Ty said, "I wouldn't mind at all."

We walked the rest of the way in silence, until we were outside the doors to the hotel. I hesitated, and so did he. I guess neither of us wanted to assume anything.

I glanced at him. "Um..."

"Yeah?"

"It's OK if you've changed your mind."

"Have you changed your mind?"

I shook my head.

"Me neither."

"So you want to come upstairs?"

"If you want me to."

"I want you to," I said and pulled him through the doors.

Even so, it was a little awkward walking into the hotel room. The sun was pouring through the French doors to the little balcony, and the ocean stretched to infinity beyond. It was very private, we were up high, nobody could see in... but there was a lot of light. A whole lot of light.

When I'd envisioned this scene, it had always been dark. And I'd imagined a bit more... passion. Being swept off my feet. Having a lot less time to think.

"It's OK," Ty said. He put his hands on my shoulders and pulled me back against him. I could feel the warmth of his chest and stomach through his T-shirt and my dress.

He slipped his hands down my arms, leaving goosebumps, and then wrapped his arms around me. His voice was warm against my ear. "Just relax. And if you change your mind and want me to stop, just tell me."

I nodded. And cleared my throat. "I like your T-shirt."

He laughed. "I like your dress."

It was a simple jersey tube with cap sleeves: basically an overly long T-shirt. It slipped over my head... and came off just as easily.

I still had my bikini on underneath—I hadn't taken the time to change out of it in the hurry earlier, and besides, there hadn't seemed to be much point when I didn't know whether I'd be going back to the pool again later.

Now I could console myself with the fact that at least I wasn't standing here in my underwear. I was wearing as much as I'd worn outside in public earlier.

"I like this, too," Ty murmured and fingered the ruffles at my hips.

I swallowed. Hard. "Thank you."

"Pink is definitely your color." There was a smile in his voice, and I wasn't sure whether he was talking about the bikini or the color in my cheeks. His hand skimming across my stomach was warm, the palm a little rough. I caught my breath fast when he flicked the ruffles on my bra with a fingertip, too.

"You still OK?" he whispered in my ear.

My voice hiccuped. "I think."

"Let me know if you're not. If you need me to slow down." He brushed the hair away and kissed my shoulder. And then the side of my neck.

I turned in his arms, tilting my face up, and then he kissed my mouth. And just like last time, my stomach turned to liquid and so did my knees. I didn't even notice that he walked us backward toward the bed. Not until the backs of my knees hit the mattress and I fell over, with him on top of me.

For a second, it was déjà vu all over again, and I froze. Until I heard his voice, warm in my ear. "It's me, Cassie."

I nodded. "Ty." I was safe. I was in my own room, and it was Ty.

I wrapped my arms around his neck and then he was kissing me again.

Somewhere along the way, his shirt came off. I'm not sure whether he did it, or I did, but I felt soft, warm skin under my hands, and hard muscles flexing and sliding against me.

And somewhere along the way, my bikini top came off, as well. I'm pretty sure that was him, because I was too busy touching him to worry about it. His naked chest against my naked breasts—for the first time ever!—was shocking and thrilling at the same time.

"You're beautiful, Cassie." He kept talking to me, soft words in my ear, little sounds of encouragement and enjoyment when I touched him. Telling me, without telling me, that I was doing it right, and that he liked me, and liked being with me.

When he hooked his fingers in the ruffles of my bikini bottoms and tugged them down my legs, my heart began to thud against my ribs. This was it. I was losing my virginity.

Finally.

Except I didn't. Not then. Instead he moved back up my body and kissed me some more, his hands exploring.

"Before, behind, between, above, below..." I murmured.

He lifted his head. "What?"

"It's a poem by John Donne. License my roving hands and let them go. Before, behind, between, above, below."

His lips curled. "My experience with poetry stops at, *There once was a girl from Chicago...*"

I laughed, and then thought that I hadn't realized people laughed while they made love.

Probably being able to laugh while you were making love was a good thing.

And then he touched me a certain way, and the laughter turned to a moan. "Oh, God! Ty..."

"Shhh. Almost there."

He left me to shuck out of jeans and—I assume—what he had on underneath. "Oops." He dove back onto the floor and came up triumphant, clutching a small packet.

"Thank you," I said, since I certainly hadn't thought to make sure we had a condom.

He smiled. "I'm gonna take care of you, Cassie. Every way."

His eyes were hot and liquid, like melted emeralds. I watched, curious and a little embarrassed, as he rolled the condom on. But he didn't seem to mind me looking, just grinned at me. "Just so you know, I was voted best endowed in my high school class."

"Really?" That was a category my graduating class hadn't awarded.

He laughed. "No. Just average."

"You look good to me," I said, my cheeks hot.

He smiled. "Thanks. You look good to me, too."

The way his eyes heated when he looked at me, I couldn't doubt he meant it.

"C'mere." I opened my arms, and he crawled in, his hand tracing patterns on my stomach, and then up to circle my breasts before trailing back down again. It was hard to keep focused on the conversation.

"You're absolutely sure about this, right? Because we're

pretty much at the point of no return. If you're gonna tell me no, now's the time to do it."

"I'm positive," I said. "I want you. Now. Please."

"Then you can have me. Now. Please." He moved so he was on top of me, and then so he was on his knees between my legs. I watched, my breath hitching, as he leaned forward. The tip of the condom nudged between my legs. "Relax," Ty murmured. "I don't wanna hurt you any more than I have to."

"It probably won't hurt at all." I had to take a couple of breaths while he pushed his way inside. "I've been... oh, God, Ty..."

"Sorry. Sorry..."

"No." I shook my head on the pillow. "No, it doesn't hurt. Really. It's just tight. Really, really..."

"Tight. Yeah." He had drops of sweat on his forehead.

I laughed weakly. "Thanks for doing this."

"It's a dirty job," Ty managed, his face contorted with something halfway between laughter and pain, "but someone's gotta do it."

And then he was all the way in, and we both held our breath for a moment while we adjusted.

He hadn't looked enormous earlier, but he felt enormous now. My insides burned and stretched, and I had a hard time catching my breath. Meanwhile, he seemed to be having problems of his own. The muscles in his arms were standing out—nice muscles, nice arms—and he had his eyes squeezed shut. "God, Cassie." His voice was strained. "I gotta move. If I don't move..."

"Then move," I said.

He moved. And my eyes rolled back in my head. "Oh, God..."

He moved again.

"Oh, God. Ty..."

He laughed breathlessly. "Good?"

"The best. Again. Please."

He did it again. And again. And then he slipped a hand

between us and touched me. I gasped, my body clenching around him, and heard him groan. "Cassie. Shit..."

"What?"

"Can't wait."

Then don't.

I wanted to say it, but I couldn't. Everything was coming together. The way he was moving, the way his fingers slipped and slid between us, the feel of his muscles bunching and releasing against me. My insides tightened, spiraled.

"Oh!" I opened my eyes wide. "Oh, Ty...!"

And then everything exploded, and I gasped and shuddered, and Ty muttered something, something I didn't catch because I was too busy blinking up at the colored confetti raining down, and just a couple seconds later he stiffened too, his rhythmic movements becoming jagged and uneven, his breath catching in his throat.

He collapsed on top of me, his face buried in my neck and his breath hard against my skin, his own skin slick with sweat. I wrapped my arms around him and smiled.

EPILOGUE

He was gone when I woke up the next morning. Part of me had expected it. I guess he hadn't looked forward to saying goodbye any more than I had, and this way we didn't have to.

I had hoped for a note, though. Thanks. Or maybe even, Here's my number, if you ever find yourself in D.C.

But there was no note and no number. So maybe he'd wanted a clean break. He probably didn't feel the same about me that I felt about him. He'd probably had lots of one-night stands. A guy didn't get that good without considerable practice.

I got up and showered, a little unhappy about washing the scent of him off me. It was all I had left to remind me. But while me walking into the lobby smelling like sex might make Mackenzie happy—I'd gotten laid during spring break; whoop!—I figured no one else would probably appreciate it.

So I showered, and got dressed in comfortable clothes for the trip, tossed the rest of my belongings into the suitcase, and headed downstairs in time to meet the others.

Ty wasn't in the lobby. I hadn't expected him to be, but I'd hoped.

And he wasn't at the airport, either. Nor did he call. We got on the plane to Chicago without me having heard a word from him.

The others left me mostly alone. They could tell something was wrong. And Quinn wasn't happy, either. She—sweet, loving Quinn, with an almost infinite capacity for seeing the best in people—refused to forgive James—Ivy League Dude—for lying to her about the bet. She must have fallen for him even harder than I'd realized, to be so hurt.

Mackenzie was happier. She and Austin had worked things out, and were making plans for the summer. There was talk about him moving to Chicago, or about Mackenzie transferring to Miami to be closer to him. I didn't want to lose one of my best friends, but I was happy she was happy, since it was nice that one of us was.

And anyway, there was a chance it wouldn't last. Austin was staying in Key West, and summer was still a long way off, so things could change.

Pardon my cynicism, but I was in a bad mood.

I had been looking forward to losing my virginity. I'd made sure I'd done it with a guy I liked. I'd done everything right. I wasn't supposed to be miserable.

As the plane circled over Chicago and the lake—smaller and less blue than the Gulf of Mexico—I tried to tell myself that it was OK that I'd slept with a guy I'd never see again. People did it all the time. It was no big deal. But as we headed for the runway, and the plane jerked as the landing gear engaged and the wheels popped out of the fuselage, I couldn't bring myself to believe it.

Things went back to usual the next week. Classes, assignments, hours in the library, more hours on the computer pounding the keys. Exams were coming up.

My life didn't change much. As one week slipped into the next, and April became May, I stopped thinking about Ty every minute, and stopped waiting for the phone to ring. He didn't have my number, so why would it?

And the fact that I no longer had 'virgin' tattooed across my forehead didn't change anything, either. I guess maybe the problem hadn't been the invisible tattoo, after all, because nobody paid me any more attention now than they had before I'd had sex.

I wrote an article about what happened in Key West for the school newspaper, and thought about switching my major from English to journalism.

With just a year to go until graduation, it didn't make a whole lot of sense, I guess, but I'd chosen to major in English Lit as an excuse to spend most of my time with my nose in a book. After living a little—even if it had been scary living—I thought maybe it was time to look a little farther outside myself.

A couple of girls came up to me after the article ran and told me I had helped them be more careful, so that was nice. And as Ty had told me once, it felt good to feel like maybe I'd made a difference.

I was on my way across the quad from the library one afternoon in late May when I saw a guy coming toward me. Medium height, hair somewhere between dark blond and light brown, dressed in jeans and a T-shirt.

There wasn't anything unusual about that. The University of Chicago was full of guys of medium height, with dark blond or light brown hair, dressed in jeans and T-shirts. I was dressed in jeans and a T-shirt myself, and so was practically everyone around me.

There was something about this guy, though...

My heart started picking up speed as I moved closer to him. Was it...?

He was looking around, hands in his pockets, and hadn't seen me yet. A couple of girls walking in front of me passed him, and looked back over their shoulders with appreciative smiles.

When he got closer, I saw that the T-shirt—dark blue—

said *FBI* in large letters. I had to get all the way up in front of him to read the small letters below: *Female Body Inspector*.

By then, the question of whether it was Ty had already been answered.

He stopped in front of me. "Hi."

He looked a little nervous, like maybe he wasn't entirely sure of his reception.

I smiled. "Nice shirt."

He glanced down at it, and back up at me. "Thanks."

"Wanna inspect my body?"

"Yeah," Ty said, and reached for me.

Want more Sex on the Beach?

BEYOND ME
By Jennifer Probst

CAN FUN IN THE SUN TURN INTO LASTING LOVE?

Spring break in Key West with my besties was supposed to be casual fun. But I never expected to meet him. Sex and frolic? Yes! A relationship? No. But his hot blue eyes and confident manner drew me in. And when he let me see the man behind the mask, I fell hard, foolishly believing there could be a future for us. Of course, I never considered our relationship might be based on lies...or that his betrayal could rock my foundation and make me question everything I believed in…

OR WILL A LIFE BUILT ON LIES RUIN EVERYTHING?

The moment I saw her I knew I had to have her. She hooked me with her cool eyes and don't-touch-me attitude. I had it all—money, social status, and looks. I could get any girl I wanted...until her. When my friends challenged me with a bet to get her into bed by the end of the week, I couldn't pass it up. But sex wasn't supposed to turn into love. She wasn't supposed to change me, push me, and make me want more for myself. She wasn't supposed to wreck me in all ways. And now, if I can't turn my lies into truth, I just might lose her forever...

BETWEEN US
By Jen McLaughlin

I'm just a girl...

I'm a famous country star who's spent her life cultivating a good girl persona to avoid bad press, but I've reached my limit. I'm going away for spring break with my two best friends from college, and we've vowed to spend the vacation seeking out fun in the sun—along with some hot, no-strings-attached sex. The only thing I needed was the perfect guy, and then I met Austin Murphy. He might be totally wrong for me, but the tattooed bad boy is hard to resist. When I'm in his arms, everything just feels right.

And I'm just a guy...

I'm just a bartender who lives in Key West, stuck in an endless cycle of boredom. But then Mackenzie Forbes, America's Sweetheart herself, comes up to me and looks at me with those bright green eyes...and everything changes. She acts like she's just a normal girl and I'm just a normal guy, but that couldn't be further from the truth. My past isn't pretty, you know. I did what I had to do to survive, and she'd run if she learned the truth about my darkness. But with her, I'm finally realizing what it's like to be alive. To laugh, live, and be happy.

All good things must come to an end...

About the Author

New York Times and USA Today bestselling author Jenna Bennett writes the Do It Yourself home renovation mysteries for Berkley Prime Crime and the Cutthroat Business mysteries for her own gratification. She also writes a variety of romance for a change of pace. For more information, please visit her website, www.jennabennett.com

This paperback interior was designed and formatted by

www.emtippettsbookdesigns.blogspot.com

Artisan interiors for discerning authors and publishers.